Books by Steven Fox
in the Linford Mystery Library:

LEGACIES
THE MISSING NEWLYWEDS
DATA HUNTER

LONELY BUSINESS

Herbie Vore, mystery writer and recent widower, leads a lonely, uneventful existence — until he begins to receive threatening postcards and packages referring to Cindy, his crush from long ago. When a teenager arrives at his door claiming to be the son of his old flame, Herbie learns that Cindy has also been receiving mysterious notes and phone calls. Who could want to harm them after all these years — and why? The investigation will uncover more than Herbie ever imagined — and possibly cost him his life . . .

STEVEN FOX

LONELY
BUSINESS

Complete and Unabridged

LINFORD
Leicester

First published in Great Britain

First Linford Edition
published 2019

A catalogue record for this book is available
from the British Library.

ISBN 978–1–4448–4016–2

Published by
F. A. Thorpe (Publishing)
Anstey, Leicestershire

Set by Words & Graphics Ltd.
Anstey, Leicestershire
Printed and bound in Great Britain by
T. J. International Ltd., Padstow, Cornwall

This book is printed on acid-free paper

1

The alarm went off at 7:45 a.m. It was time to start a new day.

Herbie Vore had come to loathe getting up. It was the same routine every day and, since his wife had passed away, no one and nothing to break up the monotony.

'Get up. Shower, shave, etc., and then have breakfast,' he told himself. 'Spend time on the latest novel until lunch. Then go to the library and research the latest fiction and newspapers for new ways to create mayhem.'

Along with hating doing the same things day after day, Herbie hated his name. 'Herbie Vore,' he'd say with disgust. 'Sounds too much like 'herbivore'! What a name for a writer of mystery novels!'

And so he used the pen name of 'Henry More.' His books had always done well in the marketplace. All of his published works were a part of his extensive personal library.

Life was more exciting when Julie was

still alive, he reminisced. She had good insights to share about the plotlines, too.

He sighed and said to his memories, 'I miss you, Julie.'

★ ★ ★

'The Mouth,' Herbie's hero in most of his books, had just been hit with a sap from behind and then tied up by the gang he was chasing. The Mouth's fellow operatives only had a vague idea as to where he had gone. He had been gone long enough that his associates were becoming concerned.

'I wish the Mouth wouldn't be so secretive about these cases,' Herbie wrote the dialogue. 'He won't even tell his closest friends his real name.'

'At least his note said that he should be back by now,' another character remarked. 'Maybe we should go looking for him.'

'Any idea where we should start, Dick?' the first character, who went by the moniker of 'Mack,' asked.

'He seemed mighty interested in that warehouse by the bar on the wharf.'

Herbie was getting into the flow of the story now. The Mouth would be threatened and beaten before Dick and Mack rescued him. The gang would escape, but their questioning of the Mouth would eventually lead him and his team to the place where the bad guys were going to complete their nefarious plans.

Just as Herbie was deciding to go out for lunch, the doorbell rang. A messenger service had a package delivery for him.

'Gotta have you sign for this,' the messenger said as she held out her electronic tablet.

When Herbie had signed, the messenger handed him a package that looked to be about the size of a trade paperback book.

Since he had no projects waiting for printing, he decided to take the package to the local diner with him and open it there.

Surely some wannabe author is trying to get my endorsement for a self-published work, he mused. *Or perhaps a new publisher wishes to reprint one of my novels.*

Herbie drove to his usual eatery and ordered his usual lunch. After the waitress had served his coffee and had taken his order, he opened the package.

As he had thought, it was a book. It was professionally bound in a black and red cover, but without any title or author's name. His curiosity aroused, he opened it. Inside, except for the title page, it was filled with blank lined pages.

'What Will Happen to Cindy?' was all that was written on that single unlined sheet. Underneath the words was a drawing of a stick figure of a girl watching a childish rendering of ducks in a pond.

As he looked at the package for a return address, a duck's pinfeather that had been caught in the folds of the wrapping paper fell out on the table.

This must be a cruel joke! he thought, no longer curious, but angry. Just the week before, someone had dropped a crudely printed card with the words 'Do you remember Cindy, Mr. Vore?' in his mail slot about suppertime.

The only Cindy he remembered was the girl in middle school who had been his first crush. They had never gone far beyond just holding hands while walking home from school together. When they were in high school, Cindy had several boyfriends but always had time to say 'hello' to him. She never seemed to have any more affection for him than that of a good friend or a beloved brother.

Cindy had eventually married and moved away. They had kept in touch for a while, sending birthday greetings and Christmas cards, even after Herbie had married Julie, until one day the card that he had sent her upon the birth of her child was returned with 'Undeliverable, Address Unknown' stamped upon it. He never heard from her again.

Why was he getting these messages now? The wrapping paper's mailing label only included his address without a return address or addressee.

His lunch came and he ate without tasting it. As he looked at the title page again, he remembered that Cindy always liked to stop and feed the ducks in the park on their way home.

'This must be from someone who knew

her back then,' he said in a low voice as he pushed back his empty plate and finished his coffee.

Picking up the package and going to the cashier to pay his check, he decided to visit his friend at the police department and tell him everything he knew. He now wished that he had kept the card from the previous week, but the book and the wrapping paper would have to do.

He was not surprised when Detective Wright frowned and told him that the package might not be very helpful.

'It's a standard pre-printed label. The paper has probably been handled several times, and the shipping mark only tells us which of the company's offices it was sent from.'

'I had to sign for it,' Herbie told Wright. 'Could the receipt record give any clues?'

'That would depend on the questions that the company asked for on their shipping records,' Wright answered. 'I'll ask them for you. Discreetly, of course.'

'Of course.'

2

Early that evening, Herbie heard the flap on the mail slot as someone pushed something through. Herbie quickly rushed to the window, hoping to catch a glimpse of anyone leaving the front of the house.

Not seeing anyone, he used up his quota of expletives for the day. He picked up the envelope lying on the carpet.

Just hold it by the corner, he told himself. Now he needed to find some way of opening it without leaving his fingerprints or smearing any that might have been left by the person delivering it.

Going to the kitchen, he retrieved a sharp knife from a drawer and the box of latex gloves that Detective Wright had given him, putting on the gloves and then holding the envelope in place while he used the knife to slit the flap open. Carefully, he drew out the contents. There were two photos of Cindy inside: one a middle school photo from the yearbook, and the other taken at her wedding.

He almost missed the third photo. It was a shot of him and Cindy at the Spring Fling dance during their last year in middle school. The shot showed several couples on the dance floor. Somehow, he had managed not to step on Cindy's toes during the dance that night. It had been the happiest night of his young life.

He checked the envelope once more for a note or other message. He finally found the message when he turned the photos over. On the back of the pictures, the letters from different magazines and newspapers spelled out, 'No longer happy unless you act. Wait for next contact.'

Herbie immediately called the local precinct and asked for Detective Wright. After giving his name and the reason for his call, he was connected with Wright's desk.

'Detective John Jones,' Wright's partner answered.

'This is Herbie Vore, Detective Jones. I need to speak with Detective Wright about a matter I related to him earlier today.'

'He just left for the day. Is this in

relation to the package you left with him?'

'Yes, it is.' Herbie told Jones about the envelope that had just been left in his mail slot and what was inside. 'I haven't heard from Cindy in over fifteen years.'

'Okay, Mr. Vore.' Jones sounded concerned. 'I'll leave a message on his pager and in his voice mail. One of us will be in touch.'

★   ★   ★

Herbie had trouble sleeping that night. His mind kept turning over the package, the unposted postcard, and the letter that had been delivered in his mail slot after hours.

Who did we both know when we were in school together? he kept wondering. *Who would want to hurt either of us after all of these years? Was there someone jealous of our relationship, even as platonic as Cindy kept it?*

Sleep finally overcame him in the early morning hours as he wrestled with the demons that the recent events had conjured.

The return of his note of congratulations when Cindy's child was born had hurt him for some time. Julie, with her usual love and understanding, had done her best to console him. She had never seemed to be jealous of Herbie's affection for Cindy.

'Your loyalty to the past shows me just how sensitive and caring a man you are,' she would tell him when he asked her why she never seemed to envy or resent his lingering feelings. 'Besides, she belongs to your past and I belong to your present and your future. The one has made the others the sweet reality that they are.'

Herbie had never missed Cindy the way he had Julie when she had the stroke that had taken her life. Cindy had been an important part of his life, but he realized every day that Julie had been, and always would be, an essential part of his being.

'She would have been a wonderful mother,' he told himself once more as he prepared his morning coffee and a simple breakfast of hot cereal. 'She always seemed wistful around children after we

10

were told that we couldn't have children of our own: the adoption process seemed to drag on forever. And now it's too late.'

His melancholic mood was broken by the buzzing of his cell phone. 'Henry More,' he answered, as always, with his pen name.

'Herbie,' Detective Wright's voice greeted him. 'John left a message for me saying that you'd received another mysterious delivery last evening.'

'Yes,' Herbie replied. 'Two photos of me and Cindy from our school days, and one of her wedding with a note pasted on the backs.'

'Do you have them secured?' Wright inquired. 'Is whatever evidence that might be there untainted?'

'Yes and yes. I used the gloves you gave me and handled everything by the corners. I used a sharp knife to slit open the envelope. After I saw what it contained, I put it all in a clear plastic re-sealable storage bag.'

'Very good, Herbie,' Wright told him. 'Your research for your books will be a great help with the investigation.'

After Wright had made sure that Herbie would be home for a while, he hung up the phone and left Herbie to his breakfast and to his ponderings.

With his own mystery to solve, Herbie's involvement in the doings of the Mouth and his associates was unproductive. 'Until I know what's going on with my own mystery,' he said to the manuscript on his desk, 'I can't seem to concentrate on fiction.'

Pacing the floor as he waited for Wright, Jones, and, very probably, a forensics team to arrive, Herbie decided it would be more productive to make sure that a full pot of fresh coffee was ready.

'I've never known Detectives Wright and Jones to turn down a freshly brewed cup,' he told himself as he measured the ground coffee into the coffee maker's basket and filled it with water.

As the coffee was brewing, his doorbell rang. Thinking that the detectives had arrived, he opened the front door.

'There's coffee brewing in the machine,' he said. Instead of seeing his friends, there stood a young man in his mid-teens. Although the boy was a stranger, his features tugged at his memories. He was nearly as tall as Herbie, slender, but not skinny, with hazel eyes and dark blond hair.

'Are you Herbie Vore?' the youth asked tentatively.

'And who might you be?' Herbie answered with his own question. 'You seem a little young to be among my known associates.'

'My mother knew a Herbie Vore when she was younger than I am,' the youth told him. 'She's been getting strange notes and phone calls that she won't talk about. But I know that she's worried 'bout 'em.'

'What about your father?' Herbie kept the boy on the front steps. 'What does he think?'

'Pop passed away last winter from the flu complicated by asthma problems.'

'I'm truly sorry to hear that, young man.' Although Herbie was indeed sorry, he wanted the answers to two questions. 'But you still haven't told me your name, or your mother's.'

'My name is Johann Schmidt,' he told Herbie. 'And you knew my mother as Cindy Martin. I left her a note. I told her

13

that I was going to seek your help.'

'Before we do anything else,' Herbie commented as he stood away from the door and invited the boy in, 'you're going to call your mother, tell her that you reached my home safely, and then let me speak with her.'

As they walked into Herbie's study to use the phone on his desk, Johann told him that after his father died, he and his mother had moved to a smaller house in the neighboring city.

'I hope the phone call won't cost you anything, Mr. Vore,' Johann explained. 'The battery in my cell phone is dead. Mom would be very upset with me if I made you pay for the call.'

The youth made the phone call to his mother and spoke a moment with her, and then handed the receiver to Herbie.

'I'm sorry that Johann intruded into your family life this way,' Cindy's familiar voice said as soon as he had said hello. 'He's always been impetuous, like his father. How's Julie? Do you have any children?'

'Julie passed away a couple of years ago,' he told her. 'And no, we were unable

14

to have children.'

'I'm sorry to hear that, Herbie,' Cindy responded with a sad note to her voice.

Not wishing to give any further information about his private sorrow, he said, 'From what Johann's told me, the strange notes and phone calls may be related to events that have been happening to me during the last week.'

'Someone's been bothering you, too?'

'Possibly the same person, Cindy. Why don't you and Johann join me for lunch and we can compare notes. A couple of my detective friends are on their way over. As a matter of fact, I thought that they were who were at the door when your son arrived.'

Cindy was silent for a moment. 'All right, Herbie. It'll take me a few minutes. Could you give me your address?'

Herbie did and then he disconnected. Having been made curious, he asked Johann how he had known his address when his mother hadn't.

'I found it on the internet white pages,' Johann enlightened Herbie. 'If you know what you're looking for and how to phrase your search question, you can find out almost anything on the internet.'

Herbie decided to hire someone to help him protect his privacy better. As he considered this, his doorbell rang again. Detectives Wright and Jones had arrived at last.

'There's fresh coffee,' Herbie informed them. 'And I had a visitor arrive while I was waiting for you. He's in the study.'

As he and the detectives made their way to the study, he told them about the events of earlier that morning.

'Johann,' he said as they entered the study, 'these are friends of mine, Detectives Wright and Jones. I was expecting them when you rang my doorbell. They'll be interested in what you know about the notes and phone calls your mother has been getting.'

Then, to the detectives, he said, 'His mother, Cindy, will be joining us for lunch if you'd care to stay.' As he turned to go to the kitchen, he asked, 'Do you drink coffee, Johann, or would you prefer a soft drink?'

'Mom lets me to have a cup now and

again,' he replied with a note of satisfaction in his voice.

'Four cups of coffee coming up.'

Herbie took his time pouring the coffee into a thermal carafe and placing it on a tray with four cups, a small pitcher of milk, and packets of sweetener. He knew that the detectives would prefer to question the boy alone about what was worrying him. He also figured that Johann would be less self-conscious and more forthcoming with him out of the room for a few moments.

As he returned to the study, Johann was recalling how, after one of the phone calls, he found his mother in the kitchen, very pale and trembling.

'She wouldn't tell me what was wrong,' he informed the detectives. 'As I went back into the living room, I heard her say, 'If only this was one of Herbie's books, the Mouth and his friends would have this person all wrapped up in a neat package for the police within a week.' A few days later, I asked her if she had any books about someone called 'the Mouth'. She told me that she had some mysteries about the Mouth Detective Agency written by a man she knew when she was a girl.'

'Did she say how she knew him?' Wright inquired.

'She said they were once close friends,' Johann answered. 'She also said that some of the other kids used to tease him and call him 'Herbie Vore, the Herbivore.' She told me that he never liked that nickname and that he used a pen name for his books.'

'Henry More,' Herbie said, announcing his arrival. 'I thought it had a better ring to it without varying my real name very much.'

Johann spoke more about the phone calls and the mysterious letters that his mother kept receiving.

'Every one of them seemed to make her more nervous,' he told them. 'She kept talking about 'the Mouth' and how Herbie's hero would have everything solved in a week or two and the villain would be put away where he couldn't bother anyone anymore.'

'The Mouth is fiction,' Detective Jones

commented. 'I wish we *could* solve all of our cases as quickly and as often as he does.'

'The Mouth's appeal,' Herbie added, 'is that he always solves the case and gets his man.'

'Like Sgt. Preston of the Mounties!' Wright interjected. This received blank stares all around. 'Okay, I guess he was before your times. He was a character in a children's TV show when I was a kid. He was a member of the Northwest Royal Canadian Mounted Police. The shows were set in late nineteenth-century Canada. There was a saying that a Mountie always got his man. I guess I'm showing my age.'

When the doorbell rang, Herbie went to check if Cindy had arrived. When he opened the door, his breath caught in his throat. The woman he saw strongly reminded him of the girl he had known some thirty years ago, but with several obvious changes.

'Cindy?' he asked the woman on his doorstep. Her hair had begun to gray, and she was wearing metal leg braces. 'It's good to see you after all these years! Come in, please. Johann and my other guests are in the study. Do you still like Hawaiian-style pizza?'

'I love it, Herbie!' she said as walked through the door. 'Johann will eat almost anything put before him. Gee, you're looking good.' She dabbed at her eyes and kissed Herbie on the cheek.

Herbie escorted her into his study and introduced her to the two detectives. After everyone settled down and was seated, he went to the kitchen phone and called the local pizza parlor to place an order for a large Hawaiian pizza and a large Meat Lovers' pizza.

As he returned to the study, he heard Cindy explaining why she wore leg braces. As he looked on and listened, her face showed sadness, but no resentment, for her plight.

'Shortly after Johann was born,' she told her audience, 'my husband and I went on a vacation to visit his relatives in Europe and to introduce our new son. While we were in Austria visiting Erich's family, I was coming down the stairs at our hotel when the top riser gave way and I lost my balance. I fell down an entire flight of stairs on my tailbone and spine. The hotel paid for the specialists who examined me. The X-rays showed nothing had been broken, but at the time they had no way of completely assessing any of the nerve and tissue damage.

'About a year later, after I'd begun to experience constant pain and weakness in my legs and hips, I visited a neurologist and was diagnosed with moderate but permanent nerve and tissue damage. The hotel had already given me a large settlement that included payments for future medical costs related to the accident.

'Fortunately, I've remained in good health. And while I need braces for their added support, I've continued to be able to walk without canes or crutches.'

'The card and letter that Julie and I sent to you after we received Johann's birth announcement came were returned as 'Undeliverable', and I never heard from or about you until these packages and letters from non-postal sources. And then Johann showed up at my door,' Herbie told her.

'Because of my injuries,' Cindy explained, 'we were unable to return to the States for several months. We found out later that that quite a bit of our mail had been returned. I never heard from you until now.'

'And Julie and I moved here soon afterward,' Herbie replied. 'I tried resending the card and letter to the address on the birth announcement a couple of times, but they were returned both times stating that there was no forwarding address. I had no information about your husband's family in Austria.'

'Well, that's one mystery solved,' Jones commented just as the doorbell rang.

Herbie answered and found that the pizzas had arrived. He paid for them and brought them into the dining room. After he had set the table and put the soda out for his guests, he called everyone in to eat.

As they ate, Herbie compared the woman to the teenaged girl he had known. Cindy was more poised than he remembered. Her strawberry-blond hair had touches of light gray. Her face showed laugh lines more than the wrinkles of age, and her demeanor was confident in spite of the fear caused by her situation. A pride showed in her eyes whenever she focused on her son. She also showed great concern for his safety and wellbeing. He expected that after she had told him and the detectives of the communiques she had received. Alarm had shown in her countenance when Herbie showed her the package with the book of empty pages and the photos with the message on their backs.

The quick flash of anger in Johann's eyes told Herbie that the boy would need a positive way to help, or he would do something on his own that would very likely place him in harm's way with little or no hope of rescue. He would have a talk with Wright and Jones to discuss the possibilities of the boy's involvement.

His reveries were brought back into the moment when Wright commented, 'We'll have the forensics lab check these photos, and the envelope in which they were delivered, over for any clues. The book was bound at a FedEx office supply store. They get several such orders all the time. What was unusual about it was all of the blank pages. One of the employees remembered that a mannish-looking woman of an indeterminate age and physical stature asked for the book to be delivered to your address, Herbie, once the binding was done.'

'Were there any latent prints on the pages?' questioned Herbie.

'Only those of the employees who bound the book together,' Jones replied. 'This person was really careful. It's mighty hard, if not almost impossible, not to leave prints on paper. Oils and other tell-tales are too easily absorbed by the paper.'

3

By the time the detectives had finished asking all of their questions, Cindy had related how she had been receiving calls and mysterious letters for only a few days longer than Herbie. While not threatening, the calls did have an intimidating feel to them. It was the same with the items that Cindy and Herbie had received.

'Our only clue seems to be a woman of indeterminate height, girth, and facial features,' Wright said.

'Perhaps if Cindy and I went through our old yearbooks,' Herbie suggested, 'looking at the autographs as well as the pictures, we could find someone who might have had a fixation on one or both of us.'

'I'd be willing to try,' Cindy said.

'And we'll continue testing all of the materials received,' Wright added. 'Have you kept the letters that you received, Mrs. Schmidt?'

'I threw the first two away in disgust,' she told the detectives. 'But I did keep the next three. I had no way of recording the phone calls, and the caller ID was blocked.'

'Do you remember anything about the calls?' Jones asked. 'Was the voice familiar? Did he say anything that might help identify this person?'

'No,' Cindy said after a few moments of reflection. 'The voice was distorted so badly I had a hard time making out the words. I couldn't even tell for sure if the voice was male or female.'

'How about background noises?'

'No. The distortion device must have been hooked into the other phone's transceiver.'

'Tell us what he said, Cindy,' Herbie encouraged her. 'As exactly as you can remember.'

'Well . . . ' Cindy closed her eyes in thought. 'After I said hello, I was called a slut and a tease. Then the caller told me I'd have to pay for what I'd done to certain people.'

'Did the person say who these people

were or what you were supposed to have done?' Detective Wright asked as he wrote in his notebook.

'No.' Cindy shuddered. 'He or she just started yelling and telling me I was so shallow and uncaring that it was no surprise that I couldn't remember, and didn't know, the immense pain I'd caused on my way to popularity. After ranting, raving, and cursing for what seemed forever, the line went dead.'

'Why did you stay on the phone so long?' Herbie wondered.

'I was stunned. Shocked,' Cindy told him. 'I couldn't believe the horrible names I was being called, or the language the person was using.'

'Was there anything else the person said that made you think that he or she actually knew you?' Detective Jones inquired.

'Once, the caller mentioned that my boyfriend was so enamored of me all of those years ago that he probably believed I walked on water.'

' 'Walked on water'?' Herbie said in apparent disbelief. 'Those were the exact words?'

'Yes.' Cindy's face showed surprise. 'Why?'

'Do you remember the kid most of the other kids called 'the Preacher' or sometimes 'the Deacon'?'

'You mean the boy who was always telling the couples that they were damning their souls for holding hands and/or kissing?' she replied. 'He always seemed shy, not repressed, to me. I tried to be friendly, but he just couldn't, or wouldn't, connect with anyone, especially the girls.'

'Well,' Herbie told her, 'when we were seniors, some of the jocks jumped him and called him cruel names like 'faggot' and 'queer'. They beat him up pretty badly. I never saw or heard about him after that.'

'Do either of you remember his real name?' Jones wanted to know.

'It was John something wasn't it, Herbie?' Cindy answered.

'John Sommerstone,' Herbie responded excitedly. 'Didn't he have a sister about a year behind us?'

'Janah, I think her name was.' Cindy was remembering more now. 'She was kind of plain and dowdy-looking. Their parents belonged to some sect that believed that any male/female relationships outside of the family before marriage were shameful and perverse. I read one of their tracts once. They advocated totally separate schools and gender gatherings. They were against any type of co-educational comingling in the schools. It was a really strict code.'

'And since this was before the common acceptance of home schooling,' Wright added, 'their only choices were the public school system, very expensive private schools, or to just defy the legal system. Do you remember what the group called themselves, Cindy?'

'Not really, Detective,' she replied. 'I was so thoroughly confused by their reasoning that I threw the tract away and forgot about it until now.'

'I remember a group that called themselves the Abstentionist Movement,' Jones said, a frown furrowing his forehead. 'I thought they were like that Just Say No group, only they were saying 'no' to pre- and extramarital sex instead of drugs.'

⋆ ⋆ ⋆

'Mom,' Johann asked Cindy on their drive home, 'did you ever think you might want to marry Mr. Vore?'

'To me,' Cindy sighed, 'he was always a good friend. Someone I trusted like a close family member. We had a lot in common and he was fun to be with, but I never really thought about him that way. Your father was the only man that I truly fell in love with.'

Trust. A word that Johann had heard as far back as he could remember. It was a word with very little meaning to most of his peers, but one that he had seen in his parents every day of his life. When he met Herbie, he sensed that here was a person he could trust. His mother had never stopped trusting him even though she had not heard from him for years.

He believed Herbie's and his mother's explanation for the loss of contact: his parents had settled in a nice house on the plains after their return to the States. Very few of the people his mother had grown up with had with had been able to remain

30

in touch. In fact, those she had been able to reach when she returned were surprised when they heard from her. They had assumed that she and her new family had decided to remain in Europe.

'I really missed friends like Herbie,' she told him.

When Herbie's first book was published and she saw his photograph on the back cover, she had thought about contacting him. It had been years since she had known where he lived. The author's information had said that he lived in a different city from the last address she had for him. She had never been able to word her letter to him just right; and then, with all of the things that had happened so suddenly in her life — the repeated trips to specialists, Erich's illness and death — she had never gotten around to writing. Needing a sense of familiarity after losing her husband, she had moved back to the region where she had grown up. A grieving Johann had also welcomed the change.

Her high school reunion would be coming up at the end of that summer, and she had hoped she would reconnect with many of her old friends and acquaintances, especially Herbie and Julie.

When the phone calls and letters started coming, the first person she thought of was Herbie.

4

As Cindy and Johann pulled into their driveway, a lone figure watched from a nondescript economy sedan. The make, model, year, and color were like hundreds of other dirty well-used vehicles in the area. The driver wore loose-fitting clothing and a floppy hat low on the forehead. She waited for the occupants of the house to enter before exiting the car and approaching the house.

With furtive glances up and down the street, she quickly reached the door and used the heavy doorknocker. The door was opened and she quickly forced itself inside, knocking the young man who had answered the door back into the entryway.

'Johann?' the mother hobbled hurriedly back to the living room, when she heard the noise. Her son was just getting up from the floor as the intruder raised a weapon and fired at him.

Cindy screamed and the intruder fired the weapon once more, and she fell to the floor, senseless.

'Now,' the person said as Cindy was lifted from the floor and half walked, half carried out of the door, 'the next act has begun.'

Keeping an eye out for curious neighbors, Cindy's assailant got her into the car's passenger seat and buckled her in. She started the car and drove away without anyone seeming to have noticed. There wasn't enough time to go back and close the door if she were to make her escape, but that would fit into her plans perfectly.

Minutes later, the neighbor across the street returned home from shopping and noticed the wide-open front door of the new neighbors' house. Curious, she walked across to the house and called out. As she reached the porch where she could see inside, she saw Johann lying on the floor near an overturned end table. Quickly backing away from the scene, the neighbor ran to her car and retrieved her cell phone.

'911,' the dispatcher answered. 'What is the nature of your emergency?'

'I think my neighbors across the street may have suffered a home invasion.' The woman was in a near panic. 'The door's wide open and there's a young man on the floor. He's not moving, and some of the furniture has been knocked over.'

'Are you in danger?'

'I don't think so,' the woman replied. 'No one seems to be there now. I believe the young person on the floor lives there with his mother.'

Calming the neighbor as best as he could, the dispatcher asked for the address of the house and if she knew the names of the victims. On the mailbox, the neighbor was only able to find the house number.

'They only moved in a short while ago,' the excited neighbor stated, 'but I think the woman told me that her name was Cindy or Cynthia. Something like that, anyway.'

'Stay where you are, Ms. — ?'

'McGruder,' she told the dispatcher, and she also gave her address. 'Rachel McGruder.'

'Ms. McGruder, the police and a medical team are on their way. They'll need you to direct them to the house.'

Within minutes, Rachel McGruder saw the flashing lights and heard the sirens of the response team. As they came onto her street, Rachel waved her arms to attract their attention. As they pulled up in front of her house, she ran over and directed them to the violated house.

'The teenage boy is on the floor of the living room. I didn't see his mother,' she reported as succinctly as was able. 'I do know that the mother walks with leg braces. I remember seeing a kid in braces when I was in grade school. I thought that polio had been eradicated.'

The officer who had stayed with Ms. McGruder gave her a reassuring nod. 'Sometimes things happen. How well do you know your neighbor?'

'Not very well,' Rachel told the officer. 'They moved in just after the school year ended. We've talked for a few minutes several times and had coffee together once or twice. I think she said that she was recently widowed.'

The paramedics checked Johann as soon as the police had checked the front room and declared it safe. While the police checked the rest of the house for the victim's mother, the paramedics examined the boy and turned him over. The lead medical assistant suddenly pulled back in surprise and pointed out what he had just found to his partner.

'What's this?' he asked, puzzled.

'It looks like a tranquilizer dart,' was the reply. 'Be careful; there may still be some of the trank on the dart's tip. We'll let the docs at the hospital examine it and have any residue analyzed for the antidote if he hasn't recovered by then.'

The paramedics asked the officer standing guard for permission to transport the victim to the hospital and received a positive nod. Following the instructions given by the doctor on call at the hospital over their radio, they put Johann on the gurney and loaded him into the ambulance.

When the police officers found no one else inside the house and no other signs of violence, they began their routine questioning of the neighbors.

'They were friendly enough.'

'The woman seemed sorta sad.'

'The boy was very polite, but he seemed kinda lost.'

These were the comments that the investigators received. Most of the neighbors had been returning home from work and had not seen anything unusual.

'Officer,' a young girl of about twelve or thirteen said to one as he was walking down the sidewalk back to his car, 'will Johann be all right? I like him. He's nice.'

'The medical people think so,' he responded to the girl. 'Did you see any strangers near the house a little while ago? Or maybe a car you haven't seen before?'

'There was an old dirty car on the street a couple of doors from Johann and his mom's house about an hour ago. A funny-dressed lady went up to their house when they got home. She knocked on the door and went in. She came out pretty soon with Ms. Schmidt and helped her get in the car, and then they drove away.'

'You're a good observer,' the officer

complimented her. 'My name's Officer Jack. What's yours?'

'Jenny Norris. Ms. Schmidt was walkin' funny.'

'Ms. McGruder said that she wore leg braces to help her walk. Is that what you mean?'

'No,' Jenny said without any doubt about what she saw. 'The funny-dressed lady was holding Ms. Schmidt up. Kinda like she was sick or wasn't feeling too good.'

'Do you remember anything about the lady or what she was wearing? You said that she was dressed funny. What kind of 'funny' did you mean, Jenny?'

'Her clothes were all baggy and loose and were all weird colors. She had a big floppy hat that hid her face, and she wore ugly shoes. Like a nurse or a waitress.'

'Weird colors?'

'Nothing went together to make them look nice.' Jenny frowned. 'They made you feel like throwing up!'

'Jenny,' a woman's voice came from the porch of the house where Jenny and the officer were talking, 'the policeman needs to do his job. Come inside and have your supper and stop bothering him.'

'She's been no bother,' Officer Jack told her. 'In fact, she's been very informative. She's very observant.'

'Thank you, Officer Jack.' Jenny beamed proudly. 'I hope you find Ms. Schmidt.'

'We'll do our best, Jenny.'

5

Herbie's inter-city police-band scanner had alerted him to the attack and abduction at the Schmidt home. He turned on the local all-news radio station to see if he could get more details. Then he called Wright's office at the police station.

Detective Wright could only tell him that Cindy was missing and that the boy was awake and recovering, but was very groggy. 'After he was told that his mother was missing, he insisted upon seeing you. He seems to think you'll work some miracle and get her rescued.'

'What hospital is he in?' asked Herbie. 'I think it'd be advisable to talk to him before he does something rash and gets himself hurt or causes the kidnapper to harm Cindy.'

Wright gave Herbie directions to the nearby hospital. 'Apparently the boy doesn't have any relatives living nearby, and being a minor, he can't be released unless a responsible adult will take him in.'

'Could he be released to me as a friend of the family?' questioned Herbie. 'I've known his mother since we were in middle school. I've got a spare bedroom where he could stay as long as necessary.'

'Until we locate a blood relative able to take care of him,' Wright answered, 'I think Child Services will agree.'

'I'll take him to his house and let him get whatever he needs for the time he'll be with me.'

As Herbie drove to the hospital, he wondered how the teenager was processing the latest events in his life and how he would handle them.

* * *

Johann had been informed that Herbie would pick him up and take him to his house. Telling the orderly that he was hungry and wanted to wait in the commissary, he went to have a snack and to sit down.

It didn't take long for him to get restless. As he was deciding whether or not to strike out on his own, he saw Herbie crossing the room toward him.

'I'm sorry this has happened, Johann,' Herbie said when he was next to the boy. 'The doctors have told me that you were shot with a tranquilizer dart. Are you feeling up to getting a few things from your house, then staying with me while they search for your mother?'

Johann looked at Herbie curiously as he asked, 'Will I be allowed to help? I can't just sit around and do nothing!'

'If you're willing to do what I say, when I say, you can help me,' Herbie answered him. 'I'll need to know everything that you can remember about the phone calls, the messages, and the person who tranked you. Cindy said that she kept some of the messages. Do you know where she put them?'

'I saw her put them in a plastic bag and then into the center drawer of her desk,' Johann said.

'Tell the detectives at your house where to find them, and that Detectives Wright and Jones in Brookdale will need to see them because they're related to a case they're working on and may be related to the kidnapping. I'll inform Detective Wright to expect to hear from the detectives here in Riverview.'

'We're not going on the hunt for clues?' Johann sounded disappointed that they weren't going to start running out and asking questions of mysterious people like the operatives of the Mouth Detective Agency. 'Isn't that what you do in your books?'

'Yes it is, Johann,' Herbie explained. 'But you can't look for clues until you know what it is you're looking for. That takes a lot of brainstorming. Sometime for days. We'll let the experts do their job while you and I sift through our memories for anything that seems important or unusual.'

'How do we know what's important or unusual?'

'Until we've looked for a while, we treat everything as important or unusual. Nothing is insignificant until proven otherwise. Nothing. No matter how trivial.'

'So,' Johann said with a grin, 'If you're

the Mouth, which one am I? Mack or Dick?'

'Neither,' Herbie laughed. 'I'm Mack, not the Mouth. You're Yancy, the young apprentice and gofer.'

6

Officer Jack was still on duty at the scene when Herbie and Johann arrived. Johann was allowed to get what he needed for a short stay away from home.

As Johann was packing, the officer told Herbie about his conversation with Jenny. 'She was the only one we talked to who admitted to seeing anything. Her description of the car and the suspect were as good as any adult could have given. She seemed concerned about Johann. She said he was nice.'

When Johann came out of his room with his suitcase, Herbie told him about Jenny being worried about him.

'She's a lonely kid,' Johann said. 'Her parents are divorced and her mother works long hours to support the two of them. And she doesn't have many friends. Mrs. McGruder, who lives there across the street, watches Jenny while her mother works. Can we go over and let her know that I'm okay and that I'll be staying with you for a while?'

'Of course we can, if her mother will allow it.'

Johann and Herbie walked across the street and knocked on Jenny's door. When it was opened by a dark-eyed raven-haired girl, Herbie was surprised at how young she was.

'Johann!' she exclaimed. 'You're okay! Have they found the funny-dressed lady who took your mother away?'

'Jenny?' a woman's voice came from inside the house. 'Who's at the door? You know what I've told you about opening it to strangers, especially at night and after what's happened today!'

'It's Johann, Mama,' Jenny replied. 'He's home, and he's got a friend with him.'

'Johann? From across the street?' The woman quickly appeared behind her daughter. 'Do they know what happened to your mother?'

'I told Officer Jack that the funny-dressed lady took her away in her dirty of car, Mama,' Jenny said exasperatedly.

'Mrs. Schmidt didn't look good, and she was helped into the car before they drove away!'

'What else did you notice, Jenny?' Herbie asked. 'Was the lady tall or short? Was she fat or thin? Could you see her face?'

'Are you helping the police?'

'Mrs. Schmidt and I have known each other for a long time,' Herbie said. 'Someone's been sending us letters saying that bad things were going to happen. The police are trying to find out who this person is. I think the funny-dressed lady is that person, but I don't know if she's doing this alone. I think she has a brother who could be helping her.'

'Her car was a dirty piece of junk.' Jenny thought for a moment. 'Her clothes looked so awful that I almost threw up. She wore a floppy hat that covered most of her face. What I could notice of her face looked real pale. Like she never got any sun.'

* * *

'That officer was right,' Herbie remarked during the drive back to his house.

'What do you mean, Mr. Vore?' Johann was curious.

'He said that she was very observant. He also said that many adults wouldn't have done better.'

Silence reigned between them for several minutes until Herbie said, 'You don't have to keep calling me 'Mr. Vore' if it seems too formal, Johann. I'd be just as comfortable with 'Herbie' or even 'Henry.''

'Maybe after we get to know each other better,' Johann said after thinking about it. 'All of the kids back in Johnsville, Nebraska were taught to respect their elders. Unless the adult was a relative, even younger adults called the older adults by their title and last names.'

Old-fashioned, Herbie thought. *But perhaps something lacking among many of today's youth.* He decided that he liked the attitude.

It was full dark when they pulled into Herbie's driveway. Herbie unlocked the house and switched on the lights. As he turned to give Johann a hand with his

49

suitcase, he noticed the envelope that had been pushed through the slot while he was gone. There was no visible postmark or return address, simply the words 'To the Herbivore.' Cautioning Johann not to step on the letter, he went to the kitchen drawer and returned with a pair of latex gloves, a knife to use as a letter opener, and a pair of tweezers.

'Your first lesson in crime detection,' he told his guest. 'Preserve the evidence and the scene. Here's my cell phone. Speed-dial number five is to Detective Wright's direct line. Call it and let him know what we've found.'

Detective Wright answered one ring before the call would have gone to voice mail. Johann explained the reason for the call as Herbie, gloved up and, with the letter held by the tweezers, went into the kitchen. As he placed the letter on the table, Johann handed him the phone.

'Detective Wright wants to talk to you.'

When Herbie took the phone, Detective Wright asked several questions about the envelope. It was of plain stock with no stamp or return address. When the envelope's contents had been removed with the tweezers, a single sheet of copy paper and a lock of hair were the only things there. On the paper were the words, 'Phone call tomorrow noon.'

'Do you think it's from Cindy's kidnapper?' he asked, seeing the anxious look on Johann's face.

'Probably,' Wright answered. 'I don't like the way this person gets his or her messages into your house, Herbie. This person knows your routine too well!'

7

In a broken-down trailer park outside of Riverview, Cindy was blindfolded. The blindfold had been tightly duct-taped into place, making sure that no light was visible. She was secured to the bed by chains to all four posters of the bed. To further ensure that Cindy could not escape, her leg-braces had been removed.

In another room, she heard two voices arguing. It sounded like a man and a woman. 'I told you,' the male voice bellowed, 'that we didn't need to kidnap Cindy!'

'And I told you,' the female voice shouted back, 'the Herbivore needs to know we mean business! If it weren't for their false superiority and goody-goody attitudes, Mam and Pap would still be alive and you wouldn't be confined to that chair!'

Cindy thought about the conversation that she had had with Herbie and the detectives. Her captors must be John and Janah Sommerstone! She hadn't heard anything about the Sommerstone family since she had gone away to college. Why would they blame the elder Sommerstone's deaths on her and Herbie? Many of the other kids in school had treated John and Janah with cruel scorn and resentment. She and Herbie, as well as some of the others, had tried to be friendly and had been rebuffed.

Cindy heard someone come into the room. When the footsteps stopped next to the bed, she heard the person's angry breathing. The slaps stung her face, first on her left cheek and then a backhanded slap on her right.

'I've got no sympathy for a whore,' the woman screamed, 'even if she *is* a cripple like you!'

'And I only feel pity for someone as eaten up with hate as you!' Cindy responded through her bleeding lips. 'You break into my house, shoot my son, and kidnap me. Why?'

'Your bastard son means nothing to me,' the woman hissed with anger. 'You and your lover will learn the results of your evil ways when you are both punished for your sins.'

'And what sins were those, Janah?' Cindy said with a calm rationality that she was not certain she felt. 'My son was conceived in a loving marriage. Erich and I both were saddened that we couldn't have any more children after I fell down those stairs. And when he died, a part of me died with him.' Tears were flowing down her cheeks from under her blindfold as she added, 'If I deserved to be punished for anything, God's done a better job than you ever will with all of your spite and hatred!'

With an angry oath, Janah began slapping and punching the helpless woman until her brother grabbed her by the waist and powered his wheelchair in reverse to pull her away.

'This isn't the way to handle this,' he told her. 'Right doesn't need to always be represented by violence!'

Janah struggled against her brother's hold. 'She claims that she was married!' she yelled at her brother. 'A Godless woman like her wouldn't get married! Her son *has* to be the illegitimate get of a sinful relationship with that herbivore mystery writer!'

'And I think that you're out of control!'

★   ★   ★

'We can't use the lock of hair for a DNA match because it doesn't contain follicles,' the forensics detective was explaining to an upset Johann. 'The hairs by themselves don't contain enough identifiers for a match. If the hairs had been plucked out, then we might be able to get one from a sample from you. Right now, all we have are strands from someone with strawberry-blond hair, like your mother.'

'Considering the facts of the case,' Herbie asked of the officer, 'aren't they likely to be Cindy's?'

'I would say the chances are better than 50-50.'

'We'll find her, son,' Detective Wright said, giving Johann's shoulder a reassuring squeeze. 'We'll know more when they call tomorrow.'

Telephone people were setting up to record and trace the call the next day. It was an old-fashioned evidence and clue gathering device that was well known. New technology had made its use better. Even cell phone locations could now be traced and triangulated, given the time to set up properly.

'He who would do evil,' Herbie quoted from the Mouth, 'will eventually be caught in his own web.'

'I hope it won't be too late, Mr. Vore,' Johann said as he choked back his worries.

At noon the next day, Herbie's home phone rang. On the third ring, Herbie was signaled to pick up the receiver.

'Hello,' he said. 'How may I direct your call?'

'Don't play games, Herbivore,' the voice at the other end of the line said. 'I know that you and your detective friends are recording and tracking this call, for all the good it'll do you. Now listen up. If you want Cindy to be happy again, you'll make a statement in the next issue of USA Today telling everyone what a lowlife philandering idiot you really are, and that your novels are nothing but trash and not even useful as toilet paper.'

'And if I can't comply?' Herbie asked. 'What if the paper won't print this so-called confession? Or if it's past the deadline?'

'Then the next delivery from Cindy will be something more important than just a lock of her hair.' The phone clicked off.

'What did we get?' Detective Wright asked.

'PhoneStore payphone in the mall,' the woman handling the setup replied. 'A very busy place to make a call. Lots of traffic, and no one paying much attention to anyone using a payphone.'

'Now we know that there are at least two?' Johann wanted to know. 'At least one to watch Mom and one to make the call?'

'It might depend on how close to the mall the kidnapper is and how secure he or she feels that your mother can't release herself.'

'If they removed her braces,' Herbie questioned, 'how mobile would Cindy be?

Could she run fast enough to get away?'

Johann's face fell. 'No,' he admitted. 'Without her braces, she can barely stand and take baby steps.'

'So,' Detective Wright said, 'if her braces have been removed and she's bound somehow, the perp might feel safe enough to leave her alone for a short time at least once.'

'But why kidnap Cindy?' Herbie asked. 'Isn't that a federal felony? And doesn't that bring the FBI into the case?'

'Yes, it does, and Special Agents Polluck and Seth should be arriving at any time.'

Detective Jones's cell phone alerted him to an incoming call. He spoke for a few moments and then disconnected. 'The Bureau has arrived,' he told the group. 'They're waiting at headquarters.'

Herbie and Johann arrived at the police station along with the team that had been at Herbie's house. Detective Jones told them that the agents would want to listen to the taped phone call and to hear everything that Herbie and Johann knew. Afterwards, they would ask questions of

Herbie, Johann, and the detectives.

'Just tell them everything you've told us,' Johann was instructed by Detective Jones. 'And if they ask you anything you don't know, don't guess. Tell them you don't know. Don't volunteer any theories or unasked-for information. Too much input will confuse the situation. If you want to ask something, wait until you can ask me or Detective Wright. If the agents need to be asked, we'll do it. Okay?'

'You mean hide things from the FBI?' Johann asked, surprised.

'No,' Detective Jones told him. 'Just don't say anything that you're not sure of the best way to tell until you've talked to us. You don't want something that's said the wrong way to cause a bad mistake.'

When everyone had arrived at headquarters, introductions were made all around. Herbie and Johann spent the next few hours relating the facts of the events leading up to the abduction. Polluck and Seth interrupted only to ask a question or to clarify a point.

'The Riverview police report stated that after Johann was released from the hospital,' Polluck said reading from the report, 'you picked him up and brought him to his house to pack a few things, Mr. Vore. Will he be staying with you?'

'Only until a relative can be found and notified who's able to care for him until his mother can be found and rescued,' Herbie informed the two agents. 'Cindy and I have known each other since middle school.'

'Weren't the investigators concerned about crime-scene integrity?' asked Seth. 'Surely taking items from the scene and to your house would give them some problems?'

'The officer-in-charge had already checked off the bedroom and the bathroom in the house,' Johann explained. 'He okayed my packing a bag with clothing and personal items. He also assigned an officer to inventory everything that I took.'

Polluck and Seth asked which officers had taken the inventory and asked to see the items later for a comparison.

8

Janah had taken as little time as possible making the call with her demands. Ruining the Herbivore's reputation and terrifying his girlfriend seemed to be too little for the indignations and heartache the two had caused her and her brother.

I can't believe I thought that I loved him! she ruminated as she returned to the place where she and John had hidden Cindy. *He seemed so different from the other boys. And Cindy always seemed to be so friendly, while all the time she lusted after several of the boys, especially my Herbie! She only wanted him because I did! I know she trapped him into having an affair that produced her bastard. I just know that the two of them incited the riot that killed my parents. No one would have bothered them, otherwise!*

Angry tears streamed down her face as she drove. Just a few weeks before the angry crowd had stormed their house and killed her parents, several of the athletes had beaten her brother so badly that for a while it appeared that John would die. No one came forward to tell who the boys were, not even Herbie! The police were either inept, or they just didn't care that someone with such a different belief system was lying at death's door! She had begun to believe that Cindy had goaded the boys to attack her brother so that she would leave Herbie alone. She just couldn't believe that Herbie seemed so distant and cold after John had been released from the hospital. Not even word of sympathy to either of them.

She would have her revenge all right! And not just the ruining of his reputation and his livelihood! She would see him suffer as Cindy was delivered to him a piece at a time!

See how you like seeing your lover slowly dismembered! She seethed inside.

★ ★ ★

'Janah had a crush on Herbie,' John was telling Cindy while Janah was away delivering their demands. 'When I was beaten up and she didn't hear from him, she was certain he'd been turned against her. She felt that the two of you had betrayed us and that neither of you had ever been more than self-serving hypocrites.'

'Herbie told me that after you were attacked, he never heard of you again,' Cindy informed him, wanting to keep him talking in order to learn more about the years she was gone from her native state. 'And what about you, John? I heard your sister say something about your folks having died in some kind of riot.'

'It wasn't a riot! It was a lynch mob that killed them, and the police never cared!'

'But why?' Cindy couldn't believe what she was being told.

'A young couple was found dead in *flagrante delicto* out on a lonely road where some of the kids would go for their sinful rendezvous. Our parents were blamed because of their outspoken beliefs. The kids' parents and several others got together and grabbed Mam and Pap. Janah and I were hiding in the basement, but we saw what happened. Our parents were beaten with clubs, tied up, and then ropes were put around their necks. They were hung from the tree branches and left to slowly choke to death. There was nothing we could do but watch as their murderers yelled curses and obscenities.'

Cindy shuddered as John continued. 'Janah's feelings toward Herbie had already begun to turn to hate. After that, she wanted nothing more than to punish the two of you for the crimes and betrayals she believed you guilty of.'

'And how did you feel?' Cindy asked.

'Feel?' John sneered. 'First, I'm laughed at for following the precepts that my parents and my church taught me, then, I'm beaten so badly that I'll never walk again. And no one ever visited me, not even my parents! My sister was the only one who even spoke to me after my release. When Mam and Pap were lynched, I didn't feel remorse, sorrow, or any of those feelings that psychologists tell you are normal. I only felt relieved that they could no longer control me.

Yeah, and I felt bitter about how my life sucked. Especially as Janah became more and more obsessed with getting even with you and Herbie. She started calling Herbie by that name he hated; used it as an epithet.'

'Herbie disliked that name because it made him seem weak,' Cindy remarked. 'It made him think of himself as a scared rabbit. Or a placid food animal, bred to be slaughtered to feed the meat-eaters.'

'My sister began to see him as the wolf in sheep's clothing.'

9

'But it's been nearly a week!' Johann said, pacing the floor. 'Hasn't anyone found out *anything* yet?'

'This is real life, Johann,' Herbie explained for what seemed the thousandth time. 'The interview with the *USA Today* reporter was placed with the paper just as I was told to do. So far there has been no response. I think that may have surprised them, and now they're reassessing their plans.'

'Is that good or bad?' Johann quizzed Herbie. 'How would you have the Mouth handle this situation?'

'He'd tell Yancy,' Herbie said thoughtfully, ''My lad, we've played by their rules long enough. Let's change the game.' Then he and Dick would go over everything they knew, while Mack would take Yancy into the field and teach him the finer points of covert intelligence gathering.'

As Herbie was reaching for his keys, his cell phone vibrated. 'Henry More,' he answered.

'The herbivore who would pretend to be a carnivore!' the encrypted voice responded. 'I saw your statement. Now if you wish Cindy to stay healthy, you and her bastard will come to the park at midnight. When you reach the duck pond, there will be a stack of concrete blocks. In a crack between the top level and the one just below it, you'll find further instructions. I'll be watching, so it had better just be the two of you.'

There was a click as the person hung up.

'Well,' Herbie told Johann, 'we have just received new orders. It seems that your mother's kidnappers have instructions waiting for us before Cindy gets to go free.'

Detective Jones answered the phone when Herbie called Wright's direct line. Herbie explained about the kidnappers' call and quoted the instructions.

'I don't like the fact that she wants Johann with me,' Herbie said, 'And yes,

I'm sure that it was a female voice that I heard.'

'I want you and Johann fitted with trackers and wired up,' Jones said. 'We can't let this person get away with kidnapping and extortion. Celebrities face enough problems from paparazzi without some crazy coming after them, too.'

'We'll meet you at my other office in time to get outfitted.'

* * *

At 11:30 p.m., Herbie and Johann headed to the park and the duck pond.

'Technology and minaturation keep getting more sophisticated,' Herbie commented, making conversation during the trip. 'Just ten years ago, being wired for sound and fitted with a tracking device was a lot harder to disguise.

'I noticed that the tracker wasn't much bigger than a micro-dot,' Johann agreed. 'My transceiver's microphone and power unit look like a fancy bit of jewelry! I've never worn an ear cuff before. Maybe I can talk Mom into letting me buy one.'

'Better than a nose ring or a navel stud,' Herbie laughed.

The detectives were following a quarter-mile behind them.

'No more of that kind of chatter, guys,' Detective Wright advised. 'If Cindy's kidnappers have any kind of long distance-listening device, you're probably coming into their range about now.'

'Why would the kidnappers want me?' Johann quizzed. 'I'm just a kid.'

'Maybe it's a control thing,' Herbie replied. 'With you there, he or she may feel we'll be less likely to attempt defying our instructions.'

'What else could they want? Haven't we done everything they told us to?'

'A statement in a national paper under duress is too easily retracted.' Herbie had been thinking about the same thing. 'They're looking for a stronger and surer way of ruining my reputation and livelihood. And they want to lay as heavy a guilt trip as they can on your mother.'

'But why my mom?'

'Whatever I'm being blamed for,' Herbie replied as his headlights shined on the grouping of blocks near the duck pond, 'they must feel that our relationship is a part of it. At least maybe they think that by threatening her, they can get whatever kind of satisfaction they need from causing me distress.'

'Then they see me and Mom as pawns in their game?'

'Hopefully a game that they don't realize has changed its rules.'

10

Janah watched as Herbie's car stopped near the blocks. Two male figures emerged. Using an LED flashlight, the driver searched the blocks for the instructions. Meanwhile, she searched the area for signs that they had been followed or were being watched. Seeing none, but still cautious, she spoke from her dark hiding place.

'Do as I say,' her voice told them. 'Cindy's health and happiness depend on it. Walk into the pond and soak yourselves thoroughly. Take off all of your jewelry and leave it on top of those blocks. If the cops are nearby, I don't want them knowing where we're going. If I see *anyone*, and I do mean *anyone*, you, the boy, and Cindy all die. Do as I've told you, and don't try anything else.'

'Damn!' the technician inside the van snapped. 'We didn't expect this!'

'No,' Detective Wright said, 'but perhaps Herbie did. Remember the waterproof bag he asked us for? I saw him place his tracker inside and then tuck everything inside his sock. When they come out of the duck pond, check and see if his tracker's still working.'

★ ★ ★

Janah watched as Herbie and Johann placed their watches, rings and Johann's ear cuff on the stack of blocks and walk toward the duck pond.

'Wait!' she called out to them. 'Turn off the flashlight and put it with the jewelry.'

Herbie made a show of protesting before complying. When they had soaked up enough water from the pond to satisfy her, Janah picked up the jewelry and flashlight and placed it all inside the steel box and flipped a switch in the lid.

'Now you can't communicate with your friends,' she declared as she closed and locked the lid. 'The box is equipped with a white-noise device just in case any of the jewelry's being used for listening or tracking devices. The bath I made you take should have shorted any other electronic devices. Now, take the path on the right side of the blocks and follow it to the recreation center's parking lot. Get in the dark minivan.'

'We've still got the tracking signal,' the technician told Wright and Jones. 'They seem to be headed toward the recreation center's parking lot.'

'That's still within the transmission range,' Jones said. 'Sam, take us to the exit nearest that parking lot. Park where we can watch without being noticed.'

Without turning on his vehicle's lights, Sam found a parking space on the street about a block away from which he could still see the minivan under one of the trees that provided shade during the day. After several minutes, Herbie, Johann, and their captor were seen entering the only vehicle still in the parking lot. The dark green minivan chirped as Janah unlocked the doors with her remote. She ordered her prisoners into the back seat and to buckle up. After they were settled in, the woman pressed another button on her remote.

'Now,' she said, grinning maliciously,

'you can't get free until we get where we're going. Child safety locks are better than ropes or chains for keeping away unwanted trouble while driving.'

After checking to make sure they were secure, Janah took out two blindfolds and made them fast around their heads and eyes. The minivan started with a well-tuned purr, and Janah placed the vehicle in gear and drove away.

'Jackson,' Detective Jones said, 'keep our stalking horse within range, but far enough back that our prey doesn't get spooked. Keep Sam informed so that he can concentrate on his covert driving.'

When the dark minivan was two blocks away, Sam started his engine and headed in the same direction that he had seen it go. For the next half an hour, Sam followed Jackson's directions as he stayed at least two blocks behind.

'The way she keeps doubling back and forth over her trail,' Jackson told them, 'she may be suspicious of being followed or just good at losing a tail. You want me to break it off?'

Wright looked at Jones and shook his

head. 'The way she's driving, she thinks she'll spot us if she has a tail. Back off another half a block to help us stay out of sight now that the traffic is getting even lighter. Parallel her route when you think you must, but don't lose her. Three civilians are depending on us when everything hits the fan blades.'

Another fifteen minutes later, the minivan pulled into a trailer park and stopped. Janah got out and released the door and locks. After restraining their hands behind them, she led her still-blindfolded prisoners one at a time into the trailer next to where she had parked.

When Herbie, who was led in first, entered the domicile, his nose was assaulted by the stench of an unwashed body that had been left in its own filth and other unsanitary debris for some time. He heard the ragged breath of Johann as he was also brought in.

'Mom?' he sobbed, and fought to hold down his gorge. 'Have they hurt you? Do you know who's doing this and why?'

'Oh, God, Johann!' Cindy sobbed uncontrollably in helpless shame and dejection.' I was praying they wouldn't come after you, too. Using me to hurt Herbie was torture enough. But to use you against me is more than torture — it's heinous!'

'Janah's a very sick person,' Herbie spoke out, not caring if Janah was still in the room with them. 'Her illness has warped her sense of right and wrong so badly that she may never recover.'

The unseen, but expected, slap hit him like a wrecking ball. It was followed quickly by an equally powerful backhand.

'Is that what your folks taught you, Janah?' he taunted. 'Strike out at everyone and everything that doesn't fit into your rigid little box! Whatever happened to learning the truth so that you could be set free?'

Janah shrieked as she attacked him with her nails. 'You're a fine one to talk!' her voice was shrill as she continued to attack him. 'You and your whore set our neighbors against my parents the night they lynched my mam and pap! I thought you were different! I watched as my parents were beaten and brutally murdered while the police did nothing to help them! Their murderers laughed and called them vile names! Where were the two of you? Were you off somewhere fornicating? Indulging in your sinful desires while the lies that you had spread worked their evil?'

Herbie heard another, male, voice behind her. 'Stop it, Janah!' it said loudly. 'What's been done can't be undone. Torturing and killing these three won't bring our parents back or make me walk again. Yes, I'm filled with just as much anger as you are about many things, but I want justice for them, not revenge! I'm also sane enough to know that the past is unchangeable.'

'You fool!' Janah screamed at her brother. 'Those murderers have never spent a day paying for what they did!'

'Not true,' Herbie over shouted them. 'The killer of that boy and girl found on that lonely road was eventually caught, tried, convicted, and sentenced to death. It wasn't the first time she'd killed and then made it look as if the couple were engaged in the sex act when they were murdered.'

'And what about the lynch mob?' Janah asked. 'No charges were ever brought against any of them!'

'The evidence was all circumstantial, and your church's elders decided to let God punish them through their consciences, if they had any. The trial of the real killer of the two out on Lovers' Lane was proof that the lynch mob had killed the wrong people and that they would now have to live with that guilt.'

Janah's face contorted with rage and indignation as she tried once more to attack Herbie. 'Lies!' she screamed. 'You set the neighbors on my folks. You caused those boys at the school to beat John until he almost died!'

'We have to leave, Janah,' John spoke up suddenly. 'I heard cars driving slowly around the park. Herbie must've been followed.'

'No way, John!' Janah spat out her words. 'I made them soak in the duck pond and I kept an eye on the mirrors for anyone following me!'

'Kidnapping is a federal felony. Let's get out of here before they find us!'

John and Janah quickly duct-taped Herbie's and Johann's legs together and then added more over the mouths of Cindy, Johann, and Herbie.

Quietly slipping out of the back door, Janah pushed a button hidden under the kitchen counter. She had an evil look of satisfaction as she wheeled her brother into the minivan.

They'll never be found in time! She sneered silently. *The Herbivore, his whore, and their bastard will soon be nothing but ashes!*

★ ★ ★

Agents Polluck and Seth found that they had little need for stealth. The back door to the trailer was wide open and the minivan was gone. Seth radioed Detectives Wright and Jones of their findings and proceeded to clear the kitchen as the detectives came in the front door and began to clear the living room. The four men worked their way quickly to the single bedroom. There they found three victims, who they helped outside after cutting their bonds.

Sniffing the air, Johann said to the others, 'Let's move away from here! I smell gas leaking from somewhere.'

'The boy's right,' agreed Agent Polluck. 'I smell it, too! The kidnappers may have left a time bomb.'

Everyone had just piled into their vehicles and gotten a few hundred yards away when the trailer exploded in a flaming fireball. Fortunately, no one was near enough to the explosion to have been seriously injured. Sam turned on his vehicle's emergency signal lights as he was helped out of his safety restraints. Detective Jones used his cell phone to call 911 while Detective Wright told the police dispatcher what had happened.

'We'll need patrols to BOLO a dark green minivan, possibly equipped with a wheelchair lift. 911 is sending fire/rescue and medical units to the scene. The kidnappers are to be considered armed and extremely dangerous. The female suspect is reported by all three of the victims to be extremely volatile.'

The first responders arrived in record

time and began putting out the fire and providing first aid to any injured at the scene.

Later, at the hospital, Cindy was given a bath, a shampoo, and fresh clothing. She was also brought food and rehydrating drinks containing plenty of electrolytes, then given the opportunity to speak to the on-call counselor. But she declined, stating that she needed to rest for now and to be with her son. 'Perhaps later,' she told the doctors.

11

Agents Polluck and Seth met Herbie in Integration Room #2 the following morning.

'Tell us about the Sommerstones,' Agent Seth asked Herbie. 'Why have they fixated on you and Cindy?'

'When we were in high school, John and Janah were often ridiculed because of their church's almost fanatical belief that unmarried males and females outside of the family unit were not to have any close relationships with one another. When John was attacked and paralyzed, Janah, who I now know had a crush on me, began to hate me for not visiting John in the hospital or after his release.'

'Why didn't you attempt to see him?' Agent Polluck inquired. 'Several of your contemporaries claim you were friendly with John.'

'When John was attacked,' Herbie explained, 'I was out of state with my parents attending my great-grandparents' sixty-fifth wedding anniversary. When I found out about John after we returned, no one knew, or would tell me, of his whereabouts. A month or so later, two students were found killed, presumably while having sex. John and Janah's parents were blamed, and the mob took Mr. and Mrs. Sommerstone by force from their home. They were beaten, hung from a tree, and left to die.'

'What were the reactions of the younger Sommerstones?'

'John was of majority by then, so he became Janah's guardian and they moved away. Other than that, I have no idea.'

* * *

After Cindy was released from the hospital and had been fitted with new braces, she also was interviewed by Polluck and Seth. She told them what she knew about John's beating and the mob riot that had killed the elder Sommerstones. She repeated everything that John had told her during her captivity. She also told the agents about the arguments-between the siblings and Janah's ravings and unreasoning blame of her and Herbie for everything that had happened at that time.

'John seemed to be just as angry as Janah,' she told the FBI agents and the detectives, 'but he sounded as if he were more sane and able to control his emotions.'

'How certain are you that it was the Sommerstones that had abducted you?' she was asked. 'After all, you were blindfolded the whole time.'

'Very certain,' she replied. 'Not only were their voices familiar, but I heard them call each other by name several times during their arguments. Nor did John correct me when I called him by name or asked specific questions using his sister's name.'

When all of the interviews were over, Cindy and Johann were told that they could either return to their home or go to a local FBI safe house.

'I think Jenny would be less worried about Johann,' Cindy said with a grin, looking at her son as his face turned red, 'if we returned home. With school being out for the summer and Jenny's mom working all day, she'll enjoy having someone around that's near her own age for company.'

'We'll set up an overwatch,' Agent Seth said after he, Agent Polluck, and the detectives had discussed matters among themselves. 'You'll be given 24/7 protection until we find the Sommerstones again.'

★   ★   ★

Herbie looked at the blank pages of the 'book' he had been sent when everything had just begun.

He opened to the only page with words. *What Will Happen to Cindy?* the title page began. He turned to the first of the blank pages, took out his ball-point pen and wrote, 'A True Mystery.' On the following pages, Herbie wrote, in novelized form, everything that had happened since the first postcard had been pushed through his mail slot. By the time he had brought everything up to date, it was late and he decided to go to bed. *Tomorrow,* he thought, *I'll use a pencil and notepad to put down any questions that come to mind.*

He was awakened by the ringing of the landline phone next to his bed only a few hours later. 'Yallow?' he mumbled sleepily into the receiver.

'Mr. Vore?' a barely familiar voice spoke urgently to him. 'This is Agent Seth of the FBI. We have a situation.'

Herbie, now fully awake, sat up in bed as he asked, 'What type of situation, Agent Seth?'

'We have a body . . . ' he began.

'Are Cindy and Johann safe?' Herbie interrupted, hoping and praying that the unthinkable had not happened.

'They're fine, Mr. Vore,' Seth quickly replied. 'This is the body of a man about your age. He was found in an apartment about a mile from the trailer where Cindy was held. The headboard was covered with blood also. We think that he could have been one of our suspects. Do you think you'd recognize him?'

'It's been a number of years,' Herbie replied, 'but, yes, I think so.'

'I'll have someone pick you up, would that be all right?'

'Fine. Give me a little time to get ready.'

When Herbie arrived at the crime scene, he was met by Agent Polluck. 'It's pretty gruesome,' he told Herbie. 'The victim's legs and arms were hacked off, and then he was allowed to bleed out. One of the rookies had to be sent home.'

'I'll be okay,' Herbie said. 'I've walked in on some pretty bad scenes with Detectives Wright and Jones.'

The scene was every bit as bad as Herbie had been told. He forced himself to look at the body and its surroundings. The victim, to the best of his memory, was indeed an older John Sommerstone.

'Is there any evidence who might have done it, Agent Polluck?' he asked.

'Other than someone who's very angry or sick? Only that the person was obviously known to the victim.'

'There were no signs of a break-in,' Agent Seth joined the conversation. 'The victim didn't have time, or possibly the inclination, to struggle. The ME believes he was struck a couple of times while he was bleeding out. His arms were chopped off with a meat cleaver or other heavy sharp instrument, and then the legs. The perpetrator apparently pummeled the victim's face several times with an open hand. The face shows red marks resembling handprints. There's also a large bruise on the torso. The assailant may have taken out a lot of frustration or anger on the victim as he died.'

'His sister certainly had a lot of both,' Herbie opined, 'and she kept using vindictive language whenever her brother tried to calm her down with reason. What she believed, no matter what the evidence told her, was all that she would, or could, listen to.'

'One of those 'my mind is made up, so don't confuse me with the facts' personalities?'

'As far as I could tell, during the time we were being held at the trailer and what Cindy has told me about her captivity.'

The CSI and forensics people came in to take final measurements and photographs as Herbie and the FBI agents left the apartment.

'The green minivan was found abandoned in a used car lot nearly a mile from the victim's apartment,' Detective Wright informed Herbie by phone just as he was putting his breakfast dishes in the dishwasher. 'The owners claim that none of their inventory is missing. Either Janah had another car hidden nearby, or someone gave her a ride.'

'Cindy's neighbor, Jenny, reported seeing Cindy being placed into a very dirty older car,' Herbie recalled. 'Perhaps she can tell us more about it.'

Jenny and Mrs. McGruder were sitting with Johann and Cindy in her kitchen when Herbie and Detective Wright arrived.

'This is my neighbor, Rachel McGruder from across the street,' Cindy said, making introductions. 'She's the one who called 911. The young lady next to her is Jenny, Johann's friend and Rachel's next-door neighbor.'

'Jenny and I already know each other,' Herbie said. 'Detective Wright's interested in what Jenny remembers about the car you were taken away in, Cindy.'

'Jenny, you told the officer that you saw Mrs. Schmidt being helped into a car,' Wright asked. 'Is that correct?'

'Yes,' Jenny answered the detective, looking directly at him. 'It was old and very dirty. It was hard to tell the color under all that dirt, but it could have been a pale blue or even a faded gray.'

'Do you remember anything else about the car, Jenny?' Wright inquired. 'Did you see any dents or scratches?'

Jenny's faced screwed up as she tried to remember the details she had seen. 'One of the left-hand windows had a long crooked crack. Like a lightning bolt.'

'Was it the front-door window or the back-door window?' Mrs. McGruder asked, endeavoring to be helpful.

'It was a two-door car,' Jenny recalled, 'and the front door's window was rolled down, so it must have been the back.' Though she tried her best, she couldn't remember anything more until a chance remark was made about tires. 'The tires!' she exclaimed. 'They were worn almost bald. I remember thinking how dangerous they were. My mother had warned me about how deadly slick tires could be.'

'Do you remember anything about the license plate?' Detective Wright asked as he pulled out his cell phone to report on Jenny's updated information to the desk officer. 'The color or any of the numbers or letters?'

'Just that they were muddy and an older style. Yellow on blue, I think.'

'That could be helpful identifying the year of the car,' Wright said as he relayed the information.

*　*　*

In a cheap flea-bitten flop-house, a nondescript woman was reviewing her make-up, hair and clothing. As she prepared the hair dye, she carefully made her choice of a blouse, and then lingered over whether to select a skirt or a pair of slacks.

Something flattering and that makes me look slimmer, she mused. *That devil-tongued female hound turned my brother against me! I had no choice but to eliminate him! Now, because of her and that wolf-in-sheep's-clothing lover of hers, my whole family is gone!*

The woman finally chose a black A-line skirt that would match the dye job of her hair. The white long-collared blouse would help create a slim-looking waistline once it was tucked into the skirt. Rose-pink lip gloss and clear face powder added the final touches to her new look.

'Not even my own mother would recognize me now,' she told her reflection once she was done. 'All the kids at school teased me about being frumpy-looking. Well, they should see me now! If I'd dared to look like this back then, the Herbivore would never have even *looked* at Cindy Martin!'

When it was time to check out, Janah placed her luggage in the trunk of her old Camry, paid her bill, and drove to the car wash a mile away. There she had it washed, waxed, and detailed.

From the all-news radio station, Janah learned of her failure to eliminate the people that she most hated.

'The devil protects his own as long as

they are useful to him,' Elder Limestone was fond of saying. 'That's why the good die young and the evil seem to live forever.' Now the Abstentionist Church had been reduced to just a few elderly members belonging to only one congregation.

'Even my church family has been seduced by the outside world,' Janah fumed as she drove. 'The faithful fall away and the ungodly increase in number. I will strike at least one last blow for the right!'

Suddenly, red and blue lights flashed in her rear-view mirror. 'Damn,' she muttered under her breath as she pulled to the road's shoulder. 'What now?'

The two officers exited their cruiser. The driver walked up to her driver's door as the second officer took position at the rear and to the passenger side of her car.

'Good evening, ma'am,' the lead officer said. 'Do you know why you were pulled over?'

'Not really, Officer,' Janah responded politely. 'My speedometer said that I was doing the speed limit, and I don't believe that I was weaving or anything.'

'Nothing like that, but your tires are

dangerously bald, ma'am.' He smiled as he ran her license through his reader. 'I think you might want to invest in a complete new set.' He explained that the citation he was writing would not result in a fine if she were to show proof of replacement by a certain date. 'Get the tires replaced and everything will be okay. Have a nice day.'

As the two officers returned to their vehicle, Janah took several deep, calming breaths. 'The cops *still* haven't learned to see more than a few inches beyond their noses,' she grumbled as she started her car and cautiously re-entered traffic. 'A little make-up and a change of hair color and clothing style is all one needs to become invisible. They barely even looked at my license. I could have been an international terrorist for all they would have known.'

★ ★ ★

Half an hour later, the police officers received a 'Be On Look Out (BOLO)' report on their onboard computer.

94

'That sounds almost like that traffic stop we made a short while ago,' the young officer in the front passenger seat remarked. 'The tires were bald, remember?'

'Nothing came back on the wants and warrants,' the driver said. 'When I swiped her license through the reader, it came back clean, just like the DMV report on the plates.'

'How about the back window on her side?'

'There was a jagged crack on the back window, but it wasn't in a position that impeded her vision.'

'Cars can be washed,' the younger partner opined, 'clothes can be changed, and a little make-up and hair color can completely change a woman's appearance.'

'Go ahead and report a possible sighting. Be sure to give dispatch all of the details.'

12

Herbie sat up straight, looking disgusted with himself. 'The wheelchair!' he articulated excitedly. 'That's what was missing at the scene! Does anyone know what happened to John's wheelchair? All of the reports from when he was attacked stated that he was permanently crippled. He even told Janah that holding and hurting us wouldn't make him walk again.'

'And I heard the chair's motor when he moved around by himself,' added Cindy. 'So what did she do with it?'

Detective Wright quickly passed the question along to the FBI crime team.

'The FBI gang is searching the area where the minivan was found and the apartment where the body was found. The MEs and the coroners are taking another look at the dismembered arms and legs. If this is the body of a paraplegic, the legs should show signs of muscular deterioration and the upper body should show enhanced development. The docs at the morgue weren't informed that the deceased was chairbound.'

★ ★ ★

On the way back to the station, Detective Wright received word that there was a possible sighting of Janah and her car.

'She may have dyed her hair and dressed herself up,' Wright told Herbie. 'She may not have the suspect vehicle for much longer. She got pulled over because of the tires. If she got suspicious, she would probably try to ditch the car.' He added, 'She's crazy enough to be considered dangerous. If she was the one who chopped up her brother, she definitely could cop out on an insanity plea.'

'I think she's been criminally unbalanced for a very long time,' Herbie sadly commented.

'No one likes to think that someone they know could be a berserker, Herbie,' Wright tried to comfort his friend.

'What will they do when they find her?'

Herbie was afraid of the answer. 'What if she decides to fight it out with the authorities? I can't condone what she's become, but I can't help but feel sorry for her.'

'If she becomes aggressive,' Wright said, 'Whoever attempts to restrain her may have no choice but to resort to deadly force.'

'It all seems so wasteful!' Herbie sighed hopelessly.

* * *

When Herbie opened his door, he found a folded sheet of paper addressed to 'the Herbivore' on the floor near his mail slot.

Carefully stepping over the letter, Herbie made his way to his study. There, he searched his desk for the card that the FBI agents had left with him. When he found it, he carefully dialed the number on the card.

'Special Agent Polluck,' the agent answered on the third ring.

'Herbie Vore here, Agent Polluck,' Herbie identified himself. 'I just walked into my house and found a letter that appears to have been slipped through the mail slot while I was out this afternoon. This has been happening since this affair began. Detectives Wright and Jones haven't been able to determine how the notes, cards, and letters keep showing up without at least one person in the neighborhood seeing something. They always seem to show up long after the normal mail run.'

'Agent Seth and I will arrive shortly, Mr. Vore,' Polluck said. 'Given your profession, I don't believe that I need to remind you not to touch anything.'

'Indeed, not,' Herbie said as he and Polluck disconnected. Picking up the handset and getting a dial tone, he quickly called Cindy's number.

When she answered, Herbie told her about the events since he had left her house. He also told her about John having been killed and expressed his concerns that Janah might attempt to commit bodily harm to her or her son.

'I believe she's been mentally unbalanced for years,' he said. 'Without John to control her, she's like an engine without a governor. If she's found out that we escaped the explosion, there's no telling what she might do!'

13

Johann and Jenny were seated at a card table underneath the shade of an elm tree in Jenny's front lawn, sipping iced tea and eating some of Mrs. McGruder's cookies that she called 'teacakes'. Johann was intrigued at the story she told about the last day of middle school.

'And Jeremy's face turned red with embarrassment when his drink spurted outa his nose!' she laughed as she related the incident. 'Of course everyone at our table made it worse for him by drawing the attention of the whole cafeteria with our loud shrieks and squeals of laughter.'

'I'll bet it'll be a long time before anyone lets him forget it, either!' Johann commented with a grin. 'I hope that he has a sense of humor and will take it in stride.'

'Oh, he does,' Jenny told him. 'The first week of summer break, I heard that somehow he got hold of that chemical that the dentists used to use to show the kids whether or not they were using proper brushing techniques. The two kids that had embarrassed him had bright red teeth and gums until they had a chance to brush their teeth.'

'So,' Johann asked, 'no one got mad?'

'No. Even Jackie and Jo-Jo thought it was funny and felt that they'd been given their own back.'

While they sat enjoying each other's company, neither Jenny nor Johann paid any attention to the bronze-colored Chevrolet Cruze as it drove by.

'Laugh while you can,' the driver said quietly as she passed. 'Cindy's poison has passed from her to her offspring and is now infecting a new generation. And the girl is so innocent and unsuspecting!'

Janah drove to the next intersection and turned left toward the main road out of the city's suburbs.

'This poison must not be allowed to reach out for another generation,' she fumed to herself as she began to plot how she would stop Johann's advances toward Jenny. 'The girl must not be allowed to be

102

corrupted by Johann or his mother.'

Janah wept as she said, 'And perhaps Johann can be turned away from his mother's wicked ways.'

★   ★   ★

Cindy smiled to herself at the laughter she heard as she made her way across the street to where Jenny and her son were seated. She was greeted by smiles from the two teenagers who were obviously having a good time in one another's company. As she approached, she noticed a pair of folding chairs leaning against the shade tree.

'Mind if I join?' she asked.

'No, Mom,' Johann answered getting up to put a chair at the table. 'When school starts again, Jenny will be going to Riverview High as a freshman. I'll have at least one person that I know there.'

'That's wonderful, Johann.' Cindy noticed a slight blush on Jenny's face. 'And Jenny will have a friend in the upper classes. It sounds like an even trade to me.'

Mrs. McGruder joined them, bringing a fresh pitcher of iced tea and a new plate of teacakes.

'These are really good, Rachel,' Cindy said as she took a cookie. 'Where did you get the recipe?'

'My great-aunt used to bake all sorts of goodies,' Mrs. McGruder replied. 'I liked to help just so that I could smell things as they baked. Auntie taught me a lot about preparing food.' She smiled at a memory as she continued. 'My late husband used to tease me and say that the real reason he married me was that he knew that he'd never go hungry.'

'As good a reason for a lasting relationship as any I've heard of,' Cindy agreed.

★   ★   ★

Janah drove to the motel in Brookdale that she was using as her hideaway. As she parked her car, she was thinking about how she would successfully deflect what she considered Johann's sinful designs on the unsuspecting young girl she had seen him with.

'The damage done by his mother and illegitimate father cannot be corrected,' she decided as she walked to her door, 'but perhaps the potential for future harm can be avoided.'

With a sense of satisfaction, Janah relaxed as she listened to the classical jazz, swing, and big band music station that she enjoyed, and soon fell asleep.

Awakening in the wee hours of the morning, uncomfortable and with a sense of panic, she had difficulty remembering what had intruded upon her slumbers. Then she remembered her dream. Nightmare, actually. In the dream, she saw her brother's blood-splattered face and sad, accusing eyes. He never said a word. He just looked at her. Then as she watched, his arms, and then his legs, fell away from his body, blood flowing copiously from the stumps. Soon it seemed that she was drowning in blood, and she heard her brother telling her, 'No more! Not one more drop!'

Janah got up from the chair in which she had fallen asleep. She stumbled into the kitchenette and put water in the coffeemaker and put the pre-measured package of coffee into the machine's basket.

As she waited for the coffee to brew, she considered her dream. She denied the accusing eyes. If she hadn't stopped him, he would have found a way to turn the both of them in to the police and FBI. He had attempted to justify himself by telling her that what they had done, and were doing, was just a wrong as what had happened to them. 'No more bloodletting,' the dream was trying to tell her. 'Hatred and vengeance only begets more hatred and vengeance in a never-ending and even more vicious cycle.'

'No!' She screamed her denial into a bath towel. 'Vengeance *cannot* be denied! That's why I had to stop you!'

When the sun rose, she had made her decision. She would finish what she had started, no matter what the consequences and in spite of the nightmare's warnings.

'I missed destroying the mother and father,' she told herself as she packed her things in preparation to check out. 'I'll punish them by stealing their son. They'll never see him again and will always wonder what happened to him.'

She loaded the trunk, satisfied with her decision. Now to make her plans to execute her desires.

14

Special Agents Polluck and Seth were in their hotel with Detectives Wright and Jones studying the reports that had come in within the last forty-eight hours.

'I think you were right, Detective Wright,' Polluck said, 'when you told us that Janah would likely ditch that clunker she was driving. Less than six hours after she was pulled over, the car was found in an impound lot. Two hours after that, a woman matching Janah's latest description leased a bronze-colored Chevrolet Cruze from a used car lot.'

'One of our people reported seeing a bronze Chevy drive down the victim's street at around one p.m. yesterday,' Jones reported. 'It didn't seem to be casing the neighborhood, so all the officer did was note the time that it drove through the area. It hasn't been seen since and the vehicle's windows were dark tinted so there was no description of the driver.'

'In light of this new information,' Wright said, 'we'll advise all of our surveillance crew to report any new sightings of the vehicle in the area and notify the patrol officers to 'report but do not approach' any vehicle matching its description. Do we have a license plate number?'

'Yes,' he was told. 'The car dealer was very cooperative and gave us a copy of the lease agreement. Any information we may need is in the contract.'

'How did she pay?' Jones wanted to know.

'She paid cash for the down payment and the first and last month's payments when she signed the lease agreement,' Polluck said, looking at the copy that had been e-mailed to his laptop. 'She won't be able to elude us for much longer. We have too much information on her now.'

★   ★   ★

Herbie sat at the desk in his study, reviewing everything that he had written in the book of blank pages that he had received nearly two weeks ago. Using his novelization of recent events to help him be objective in his observations and theories, he wrote down his questions on a notepad as they came to mind.

'If this were a case being worked on by the Mouth Detective Agency,' he asked himself, 'how would I go about finding clues to the suspect's modus operandi? How would the Mouth and company determine her next move?'

As he pondered these questions, another line of thought occurred to him. 'Why is Janah so fixated on Johann being the product of an illicit union between Cindy and me?' he questioned, and became determined to find out. 'She's behaving like a jilted lover. Why? She never acted as though she had feelings for any boy back then.'

Deciding to learn more about the Church of Abstention, Herbie set up a search parameter on his computer. His thinking was that her upbringing and early religious training, as fanatical as it appeared on the surface, could have been behind her break with reality when all of her personal disasters had piled one upon the other.

The search didn't take very long, as there were only two hits. The first was a diatribe against any male/female contact outside the extended family and promoted arranged marriages. The second sounded like a well-thought-out apology in support of the church's precepts. The apology also contained a link to a more lenient, and not quite opposite, view.

'If,' Herbie theorized, 'it is as it appears, and Janah was raised in the more conservative position of her church, then any feelings of affection for a member of the opposite sex could possibly lead to an unsettled conflict in her mind. I need to talk to Cindy about this. She might know more about Janah than I do.'

There was an old-fashioned diner about a half mile from Cindy's house, and they agreed to meet there within an hour.

'Johann and Jenny are planning to spend the day at the mall while Rachel is having her hair done. Maybe we should do some catching up of our own, too,' Cindy commented.

As Herbie disconnected, he decided to

inform Detective Wright of Johann and Jenny's plans.

'The officer on watch told us that Mrs. McGruder and the kids had left and seemed to be headed for downtown Riverview. Thanks for providing the exact location,' Wright told him. 'Even though it'll be harder to keep them under watch, the crowds should provide them with some protection, as long as they don't leave the public areas.'

* * *

Cindy was already sitting in quiet corner booth when Herbie arrived. As he approached, she saw him and smiled. Herbie realized that it was her first truly uninhibited smile that he had seen on her face since the day her son had found his way to his door, worried about his mother.

'It's good to see that girlishly happy smile again, Cindy,' he greeted her as he sat down across from her. 'Have you been here long?'

'Just a few minutes,' she replied. 'Do you want to order lunch or just coffee?'

'I've been pretty busy,' he told her truthfully, 'and I haven't eaten yet. How about you?'

'I was just thinking of fixing myself something to eat when you suggested getting together.' Her smile made her seem younger than she was. 'I decided to wait for you.'

The waitress approached their table and took their order. After they had finished eating and were sipping on their refills of iced tea, Herbie opened his briefcase and pulled out his notepad.

'I've been trying to figure out why Janah would have such specific emotions about you and me,' he began. 'I found some information on the internet about her church and their beliefs.'

Herbie then showed Cindy the print-outs he had made of the three articles that he had found, and then continued. 'Do you know if she had any feelings for anyone before her brother was attacked and her parents lynched?'

'Remember the old cooties thing?' she observed. 'That was the class that almost all of the other kids put her in. 'Don't touch her! You'll get cooties!' they'd say back in middle school. I tried to befriend her, but she seemed to be so shut out that she avoided all of my overtures.'

'Sounds like a very lonely, totally beaten-down person,' Herbie commented. 'John was different. He seemed to be strong and self-assured. He'd state his position and let the chips fall where they would. He always struck me as being wary of others, as if he expected to be knocked down at anytime for little or no reason at all. I never could get him to trust me, or to return my attempts at friendship.'

'It wasn't as if he disliked girls, either,' Cindy remarked. 'He just seemed incapable of relating to anyone at all.'

'If Janah did have feelings for a boy back then,' Herbie finally asked, 'how do you think she would show them, and how would her belief systems have affected those feelings?'

'First, I think she would have been very much at odds with herself,' Cindy responded after considering the question for what seemed to be a long time. 'Having feelings that her church had told her were sinful and wrong, then being ostracized to the point where she never made any effort to make herself look attractive, I'd have to say that no matter who she liked, she'd fear rejection or ridicule to the point where she could only fantasize. And not necessarily in a healthy way.'

'I think I know who she had her feelings for,' Herbie suddenly realized. 'And why she took so long to exact retribution.'

'Who, and why?'

'Me,' Herbie said self-consciously. 'And she was jealous of our easy long-term friendship. She waited for an opportunity to hurt both of us at the same time. After what happened to John and then her parents, my failure to take charge and make things right seemed like a betrayal. She also sees you as her victorious evil rival. That's when her feelings did a complete flip-flop.'

'But why does she keep saying that Johann is *your* son?' Cindy wondered. 'And what would she do if she saw him with a girl? Someone that he obviously felt a friendship for? Like Jenny?'

'In her state of mind,' Herbie answered,

'she could hurt him and her badly just to get back at us. Especially if she believes that, with your 'example', he could be corrupting her.'

'Rachel should be made aware of the possibilities.' Cindy was beginning to sound frantic.

'The police and FBI are already watching the kids, but I think they should be made aware of our new line of thinking.'

* * *

'This Janah Sommerstone sounds like someone who needs a lot of help,' Jenny remarked later as she and Johann walked along the sidewalk. 'What's wrong with two friends enjoying one another's company?'

'Apparently,' Johann replied, 'she was raised to think that any boy/girl relationships outside of the family before an arranged engagement and marriage was some terribly taboo.'

'Being told who you had to marry is bad enough,' Jenny said, 'but being told who you could be friends with? Eeyue! Yuck!'

116

'A pre-arranged marriage might not be so bad,' Johann answered, 'if you had a chance to get to know each other and maybe become friends before the wedding. Everything else would be fringe benefits.'

As they walked, the two friends smiled at each other and tentatively reached out and held hands.

The bronze Chevy Cruze had been parked just half a block away. The driver's expression had gone from a neutral watchfulness to an angry scowl.

'I'm already too late!' Janah said in a growling whisper. 'Cindy and the Herbivore's poison have already claimed a new victim through their son. Now the only way to stop the spread of the infection is to purify it at the source!'

Janah sped ahead to the next street that the young couple would need to cross on their return home. Reaching her goal only seconds ahead of her intended prey, Janah spotted the female plainclothes officer following a hundred feet behind. Janah's tranquilizer gun was primed and ready with its full load of five darts. *That should be enough to let me get away with the kids*, she thought as the watch guard began hurrying toward her principles.

Janah snapped off two quick shots at Jenny and Johann, and then fired a carefully aimed shot at the guard. All three targets fell to the sidewalk. Janah hurriedly put the teenagers into the back seat of the car and drove away, leaving the female officer unconscious. Janah assumed that there was another officer nearby who would report the kidnapping quickly.

When Jenny, Johann and their guard hadn't returned when she believed they should, Rachel McGruder grabbed her cell phone and headed in the direction she had seen her charges go in and would most likely return from. A block and a half from her house, she saw a body beginning to stir on the sidewalk. Recognizing the officer who had been surveilling the teens, Rachel dialed the emergency number and explained the situation as she knew it. The officer, hearing Rachel and recognizing her, groggily gestured for the phone.

The officer gave the details as completely as she could. 'The suspect vehicle was a bronze colored Chevrolet sub-compact,' she said succinctly as the tranquilizer wore off. 'The suspect appears to have a multi-shot capable weapon. I saw both victims fall down before I was shot myself.'

The 911 dispatcher relayed all of the information and let the hospital know that a trank gun victim was on her way for an emergency examination.

Rachel helped the officer back to her car and drove her to the emergency room. The officer, whose name Rachel learned was Rhonda, berated herself continually during the trip.

'I stayed only far enough back to give them some privacy,' she kept saying. 'I thought that I was close enough to prevent any harm to the kids. I wasn't even able to get my weapon out before she hit me with the trank.'

Of course, Rachel was also silently blaming herself for allowing the couple to get out of her sight. There was really nothing either woman could have done to have prevented what happened. They could only hope that the teens were safe and would be found quickly.

15

Janah had stopped in an alley out of sight from pedestrian and vehicular traffic. Quickly, she bound, gagged, and blindfolded her charges. If they should revive now, they would be helpless and unaware of their direction of travel.

As she headed for her newly chosen hideaway, she contemplated her next set of moves. First, she decided that she needed to change cars again. Next, she needed to decide the best way to remove the girl from Johann's clutches and to protect her from the evils of modern society's 'loose' morals. Only when everyone adhered to the code of behavior that she had deviated from once to her sorrow, could the world return to the paradise of the beginning.

Johann revived before Jenny. He recognized his current symptoms from the first time he had been knocked out. Either the dose had not been as strong as the last time, or his body had been somewhat acclimated by the two doses being administered so closely together; he had recovered his sense of normalcy quicker upon awakening than he had the first time. As he attempted to free himself from his bonds, he heard Jenny begin to stir.

Working himself into a normal sitting position, he maneuvered himself against Jenny so that she could also obtain a more comfortable position.

'So,' the low-registered female voice said from up front, 'the tranquilizer's worn off. Just sit back and enjoy the ride. We'll arrive out of sight of prying eyes soon.'

I know that voice, Johann observed. *It's deeper now that she's not being hysterical, but it's her.*

He tried to find a way to comfort Jenny as he felt her tremble and heard her quiet sobs. He felt fearful, too, but he knew a little more about the person who had them under her power.

Realizing that their bonds were old rags instead of duct tape, Johann tried to put his back against hers so that he could place her tied wrists within reach of his fingers. As Jenny realized what he wanted, she did her best to cooperate.

Janah slowed to a stop just as Jenny's ties were beginning to loosen. 'Just relax while I get the door,' she said. 'I think you'll like my surprise.'

After Janah opened the door, she returned to the car and untied the teenagers' feet, then she rubbed their ankles to make certain that the circulation was restored in their legs and feet.

'Wouldn't want you to fall and hurt yourselves before I get what I want from Johann's parents, would I?' she almost laughed. 'There's a small step right in front of you now. Step up. Okay, now go forward about a dozen steps, turn around and sit on the couch. Careful, it's kinda low.'

★ ★ ★

The news that they received when Cindy made contact with Mrs. McGruder put both her and Herbie into a state of apprehension for the two innocent young people.

'Has Mrs. Norris been told what happened?' Cindy inquired over her cell's speakerphone. 'She'll be hysterical when she learns that Jenny's been grabbed right off the street in front of a policewoman in broad daylight!'

'She's been told,' Rachel responded. 'She's already making threats, accusations, and otherwise making a nuisance of herself. Hard to blame her when her only child has been kidnapped. She always half expected her ex-husband to try something like this, even though he never showed any interest in his daughter.'

'We'll find them,' Herbie spoke up, trying to encourage everyone. 'You have the word of the Mouth Detective Agency on that, ma'am.'

Cindy smiled and touched Herbie's cheek as she disconnected the call. 'Thank you for those words of reassurance, Mr. Mouth.'

'No one gets away with stealing one of my agents. Not even an apprentice as young as Yancy. We can't let them get away with kidnapping his friend, either!'

* ★ *

'Yancy', AKA Johann, was taking advantage of Janah's leaving him and Jenny alone while she switched to another car. Jenny's bonds were almost undone. The last knot came loose, and her hands were free. She removed her blindfold and gag and then proceeded to free Johann, which only took a few minutes. Johann and Jenny peered through the curtains to see if they could tell where they might be.

'Looks like some kind of park or something, Jenny commented. 'Could we have been dropped off at a retreat cabin?'

'Maybe,' Johann agreed. 'You know this area better than I do.'

'The only place like this that I know of is the Oak Leaf Acres. It's not that far a drive from where we were taken. I think it's maybe a timeshare vacation retreat, so I don't believe we can just go to the neighbors and ask to use their phone.'

'No, but the roads should be well marked.' Johann was beginning to think they could find a way out of this situation. 'Let's get to someplace where Janah can't find us right away and get our bearings. Then we can look around for a working payphone, if they still have such a thing, nearby. They seem to be a vanishing commodity nowadays.'

They took a quick look around. Fortunately, the doors could be unlocked from the inside without a key and then set to relock when closed from the outside.

The young couple did their best to stay out of sight as they sought the exit from the retreat. As they waited, hidden near an electronically controlled gate, a white Cadillac Escalade with tinted windows stopped and the driver punched in a code on the keypad. The Escalade pulled through the now open gate and disappeared down the road in the direction from which they had just come.

'Let's leave,' Johann said in a whisper, 'while there's no one on the road. We need to get as far as from here as we can before she discovers that we're gone.'

Without disagreeing, Jenny ran with Johann to the gate and then squeezed between the bars.

Johann and Jenny did not stop until

they found a small convenience store half a mile from the retreat. Spotting and old-fashioned phone booth, they soon discovered that the phone worked. Johann checked his pockets for quarters. Finding two, he put them into the slot and dialed his mother's cell phone.

Cindy, having seen Johann's cell phone on its charger, answered on the first ring. 'Johann?' she said, nearly in tears. 'Are you and Jenny okay? Can you tell us where you are?'

'That lady, Janah,' he quickly told her, 'took us to a resort or timeshare. Jenny thinks it's called Oak Leaf Acres. We're using a payphone in a booth just outside the Jan and Dean Market. It's about half a mile from the retreat.'

Jenny told him the names of the streets that crossed in front of the store and he repeated them to Cindy.

'How did you get away?' Herbie had Cindy ask.

'She left us alone while she apparently traded her bronze Cruze for a white Escalade. We escaped while she was gone. I think she came through the gate while we were hiding in the bushes, so we'll stay out of sight until you can pick us up. We won't go with anyone neither of us knows. The booth or the store should help us stay out of sight until then. The phone booth is one of those really old ones with pebbled glass. I think that we should be good hiding here for a while.'

Cindy filled Herbie in on what she had been told and then relayed a message from him.

'Mack says to tell Yancy and his friend that he'll be there ASAP with friends. He says that he's very proud of you. And so am I. Stay safe until we can get to you.'

As Johann was hanging up the phone, Jenny saw the white Escalade driving slowly from the retreat's direction.

'Get down, Johann!' she said, pulling on his sleeve. 'I think that's her! She must know we're gone by now and that we couldn't have gotten far.'

'Okay.' Johann was thinking frantically. 'We need a way to leave a message for Mr. Vore and his friends. We'll use the same code he gave my mom. He's Mack, from his books. I'm Yancy, a young apprentice he made up when he picked me up from the hospital. Maybe you can choose a name for Yancy's best friend?'

'How 'bout Nancy Drew?' Jenny responded. 'That way we're all detectives, right?

Johann made no answer. He just grinned at her.

★ ★ ★

Herbie called Detective Wright and informed him of the news he had concerning Johann and Jenny.

'I'll have the local sheriffs near the Jan and Dean Market watch for the Escalade,' he told Herbie. 'I'll meet you there in about fifteen minutes. I'll also have Agents Polluck and Seth meet us there. You take the kids to the safe house that we used last year to keep the U. S. Marshals' protectee until they had all of the paperwork done on her new ID. John will be waiting for you.'

'Thanks, George.'

Herbie told Cindy about Wright's plan as they got into his car and headed to where Johann and Jenny were waiting for them.

'I hope they are able to stay out of sight until we arrive,' Cindy remarked as she got into the car.

★　★　★

Behind some trees away from the road, Johann and Jenny waited for Herbie and Cindy.

'I hope that the counterperson recognizes them from our description,' Johann said worriedly. 'If we miss seeing them when they drive up, they won't know where we chose to hide.'

'Your mom's very recognizable wearing her leg braces,' Jenny assured him. 'That note in the sealed envelope was a good idea, too.'

The Escalade had driven by the store twice more since they had used the payphone. The vehicle's driver had gotten out to check the phone booth both times and had gone inside the market once to purchase a box of cookies and a can of soda. As she had gotten into car that time, a sheriff's car pulled into the parking lot.

'Call the dispatcher with our twenty. I'm going inside for a cup of coffee. You want one?' the driver said as he opened his door.

Receiving a negative gesture, the driver continued into the store.

Janah decided to leave. *No sense taking chances,* she thought. *Those two kids might not have used that payphone after all.*

As she drove away, the deputy came out with his coffee. 'The cashier just told me that he had a couple of teenagers, a boy and a girl, who had given him an envelope for the boy's mother and her friend,' he told his partner. 'They told him a story about having escaped from a kidnapper. He said he figured them for a couple of runaways.'

The radio started emitting their call sign. 'Two Beta Four to dispatch,' the passenger deputy replied. 'Go ahead.'

'Be on lookout for Caucasian male, dark blond hair, blue eyes, age fifteen; and a Caucasian female, blond hair, blue eyes, age thirteen, believed to have been abducted earlier today by a Caucasian female, mid- to late forties, dark hair, average height and build. Possibly now driving a white Cadillac Escalade. Abductees are

130

reported to have escaped from their captor. The boy's mother and a friend are on their way to meet them at the Jan and Dean Market in the Oak Leaf area.'

'Two Beta Four acknowledges,' the deputy said. 'We're in the parking lot now. The cashier claims that BOLOs may have been in the vicinity recently. Will investigate further.'

As the deputy placed the microphone back in its holder, Herbie and Cindy drove up, soon followed by the FBI and Deputy Wright. Everyone, the sheriff's deputies included, walked into the store.

Seeing Herbie and Cindy, Johann and Jenny headed toward the phone booth. 'We'll stay hidden in the phone booth until Mom and Mr. Vore come back out of the store,' Johann told Jenny. 'That'll give us our best chance to be taken to safety.'

'Your ideas seem to be working so far,' Jenny agreed.

The young people used the lengthening shadows to aid them in their trip to the phone booth. They had just made it safely inside the booth when they heard the market's door close noisily.

'Yancy,' Cindy called, 'Mack and I have your message. We're here to take you and Nancy to a safe house that the Brookdale detectives told us about.'

Johann peeked through the crack he had left in the booth's folding door. When he saw that his mother and Herbie were accompanied by one of the detectives he had met on the day he had gone to the Vores' address, he took Jenny's hand and led her to the waiting arms of his mother.

'Will someone be telling my mom that I'm okay and safe?' Jenny inquired with relief in her eyes.

'She and Mrs. McGruder are being told by Mack right now,' Cindy said as she reached out and pulled the girl into a reassuring hug. 'Let's get into the car. We need to get going. Janah may have been here just before the sheriff's arrived.'

'We saw her check the phone booth twice, Mrs. Schmidt.' Jenny related the movements that Janah had made while she and Johann had been hidden behind the trees. 'She left the second time right after the deputies arrived.'

'Then she could be waiting close by,'

Herbie said as he disconnected from his conversation Mrs. McGruder and Mrs. Norris, 'intending to follow us to the safe house. I'll let Detective Wright and the FBI agents know what Jenny just told us. Was she definitely driving the Escalade?'

'Yes,' both teens stated unequivocally.

Johann continued, 'She's got herself prettied up compared to what you said she looked like in Mom's high school yearbook.'

'I think that she dyed her hair, too,' Jenny added. 'She was too far away for me to be sure, but I couldn't see any gray in her hairdo. And her clothes weren't that awful mishmash that made you nauseous.'

'Very good observations, Nancy.' Herbie smiled at her as he went back to Detective Wright and Agents Polluck and Seth to let them know what they had just learned.

'We'll give you a five-minute head start,' Agent Seth told him. 'Then we'll check to see if you pick up a tail along the way. Have Ms. Schmidt take your cell. If we need to have you change direction, we'll call you. Otherwise, go directly to the safe house.'

Detective Wright walked over to the

deputies and told them about the plans that had been made.

'For once,' he told them, 'we have true interdepartmental cooperation.'

⋆　⋆　⋆

Janah had parked out sight from the market just past a curve in the road and screened by a short row of hedges.

'Those kids have more luck and guile than I've given them credit for,' she fumed as several cars passed by her on their way to and from the store. 'They must have gotten in touch with Cindy and the Herbivore after they escaped from the timeshare.'

As she sat wondering what to do next, she recognized Herbie's car drive by her.

'The righteous shall prevail!' she said to herself as she started the Escalade and got back onto the road just a few car lengths behind her prey. 'These evil ones, at least, shall be made to pay for their sins.'

Detective Wright relayed by cell phone to Cindy that the Escalade was following them and told them to proceed as if they were not worried about being followed.

Intent on the car in front of her, Janah did not see the brown sedan, the unmarked police car, or the sheriff's vehicle following her.

'Suspect is still following the subject's vehicle,' Agent Polluck said into his microphone. 'Two Beta Four, ease ahead of our subject. Brookdale One, be prepared to change position with us as we enter into heavier traffic. When we get to the safe house, everyone be prepared for any reaction from the suspect. Hopefully we can take her into custody without violence.'

Wright again contacted Cindy. 'As long as she takes no overt action, pretend that you're unaware of her presence. We know that she's willing to kill, so let's not push any of her buttons.'

With Agents Polluck and Seth coordinating their movements, the shadower was unaware of being shadowed. The parade of vehicles soon reached a community of large ranch-style homes on half-acre lots. As Herbie approached the last house on the street, He saw one of Brookdale PD's unmarked cars.

'Detective Jones is here,' Herbie told his passengers. 'Everyone act as if we're relieved to finally be here without any trouble.'

As Jones approached their car, he signaled them that all was according to plan. 'Janah's about fifty yards down the street,' he reported when he met the group as they got out of the vehicle. 'She's behaving as if she doesn't know she's being watched. Let's get into the house before she makes her move.'

Janah watched as the foursome entered the house with the man who had met them in the driveway. They were definitely under police protection. She should have succeeded in carrying out her plans before now. It wasn't the police who had spoiled her plans. It was her victims who had not cooperated.

She checked out her Thompson .45 submachine gun replica. The magazine was full and the weapon was set to fire three shots with every pull of the trigger. The safety was off and the bolt had been pulled back, setting the first bullet into firing position.

★   ★   ★

The FBI agents and Detective Wright had circled the block and entered the house from a pathway that hid them from Janah's sight. They were just getting into place when the two sheriff deputies reported that Janah had started her car and driven away.

'What's she doing?' Cindy wondered aloud. 'Is she giving up?'

'Not her,' Herbie replied. 'She knows we must have at least one protector. I think she'll be back when she believes our guard's changing shifts so she can catch everyone unaware. What do you think, George?'

'I think that's just as likely a scenario as any,' the detective replied. 'She keeps acting unpredictably and she keeps ratcheting up the violence.'

16

Janah had decided to wait until the shift change at midnight. She had read that the best time to catch someone unaware was at three in the morning because the human biorhythm was supposedly at its lowest and most vulnerable at that time. She believed, however, that when people were going off and coming on shift, they would be less attentive to their surroundings and therefore more likely to be taken by surprise.

It's a good plan, she had convinced herself. *Even if I die, I'll be able to take all of those sinners with me to hell!*

Glancing at her watch, she placed extra magazines in her sling pouch's pockets, checked the settings on her weapon, and got into her SUV.

'Tonight will be the end of everything!' she said as she started her vehicle. 'No more guilt from not following what I've been taught! No more shameful memories!'

* * *

'She should be coming soon,' Agent Polluck said as he paced back and forth. 'She hasn't been a person to show much patience beyond the immediacy of the plan.'

'She's waited nearly twenty years, Agent Polluck,' Herbie reminded him. 'I'd say that shows a lot of goal-oriented patience. Waiting and planning so that everything would finally fall into place, and then executing that plan precisely.'

'He has a point, Jeff,' Agent Seth added. 'She really hasn't fit any profile on file.'

'That may be true, Jake,' Polluck answered, 'but she's shown a pattern for impetuousness.'

'All of which makes her an unpredictable danger,' Herbie reminded everyone.

As the midnight hour approached, everyone in the safe house became more and more on edge.

'What if she's chosen the time when alertness is at its lowest?' Johann asked. 'Isn't that supposed to be around three a.m.?'

'That's why I made sure that deputies

will be making a point of patrolling at midnight and again at three,' Detective Wright said. 'More attention at those times should help catch anything unusual.'

Agent Seth's cell phone vibrated. 'Yes?' he said as he put the phone to his ear. 'All right, we'll be ready. Thanks.' Ending the call, he turned to the others. 'Looks like it's about show time. The Escalade has been seen parked down the street. Cindy, you and Herbie take the kids and lock yourselves in the panic room until you receive the 'all clear' from one of us. Don't let anyone into that room who isn't anyone of us.'

The deputies, on patrol through the ranch home estates, had seen the white Escalade parked next to the curb two homes away from the safe house with no one inside.

After notifying their dispatcher that they were going to be on foot patrol, the deputies parked their vehicle behind the luxury SUV, locked up the patrol car, and got ready to seek the backyards for their suspect.

'There are a lot of trees and bushes where she can hide,' the senior deputy told her partner. 'I'll break out the IR goggles. Maybe we'll get lucky and spot her heat signature.'

Just as her line of sight of her partner was hidden by the trunk's lid, a figure that had blended in with the shadows cast by the house quietly came up behind her. Using a steel-cored wooden baton, the person hit the unsuspecting deputy just behind the ear and caught her, lowering her gently to the ground.

From behind the trunk lid, the assailant called out in a loud whisper, 'These goggles are all tangled up. Come help me with them.'

As the other deputy rounded the rear of the car, he was hit across the bridge of his nose. He fell to the ground, on the verge of passing out, and a well-placed blow the temple finished putting him to sleep. Taking the Taser pistol from the deputy's belt, the female assailant shot both of the downed deputies.

That should keep them out of the way until I'm done. She angrily kicked both deputies in the ribs and then their heads. *That's to teach you to watch your backs!*

Quickly wiping down the non-lethal police weapon she had used, she took her baton and returned it to the storage compartment of the Escalade. Retrieving her sub-machine gun, she quickly and silently melted into the night.

★　★　★

Detective Wright had shown the four civilians to the basement's panic room and explained its locking mechanism.

'The door can only be opened from the inside after you set the lock,' he explained to them. 'We can give the 'all clear' through the intercom here. Do you have a code you'd like to use to let you know that it's one of us?'

''Lucy, I'm home!'' Herbie laughed.

'That'll work.' Wright had a smile on his face as he returned upstairs.

Detective Wright informed the others of the recognition code and then returned to the basement with Detective Jones.

★　★　★

Janah had taken her time working her way to bring the rear entrance of the safe house into view. She soon determined that there was no one patrolling the outside perimeter.

'A trap?' she asked herself as she watched. 'Or just a momentary lack of manpower?'

Either way, she needed to complete her plan quickly. She had no idea what the two deputies had communicated before she took them down. She estimated that she had no more than another forty-five minutes before the deputies would be found, just waking up from their enforced nap.

The bruises would validate their tale of being attacked by an unseen person. She figured that getting the tale told and then relayed to the team inside the house would add another five minutes. *Plenty of time to take down the guards*, she mused, *and then to find and dispatch the others. After that, I don't care what happens to me.*

As Janah envisioned her victory, Agent Polluck was having a worried discussion with his partner. 'I don't like not hearing from those deputies, Jake,' he said. 'They should've told us something by now.'

'I agree, Jeff.' Agent Seth unconsciously tugged at his ear. 'I'll text their cell and ask for an update.'

'While you do that, I'll get their dispatch to have someone check their last reported position.'

Agent Polluck was talking to the Oak Leaf sheriff's substation when several shots were fired through the back door and the kitchen windows.

'Federal agents have been fired upon!' he said rapidly into the phone. 'Special Agents Polluck and Seth requesting assistance at this location ASAP, if not sooner!'

Taking cover behind the heaviest furniture they could find, both agents got ready for the battle of their lives. The fact that the shots had penetrated a three-inch solid hardwood door like soft butter told the men that their attacker was using illegal loads.

Detective Jones, hearing the gun play, had approached the stairs. Hearing the agents calling to each other, he quickly closed off the staircase.

'Get under cover, George!' he told his

partner. 'The FBI agents are taking heavy fire. It sounds like they're outgunned.'

Wright pushed the intercom button and warned his charges about what was happening. 'Stay inside until you're given the password,' he commanded them.

The sounds of battle from upstairs went silent for several seconds, then started up again in a sporadic fashion. When everything was quiet again, the two detectives waited to hear if the agents had survived their ordeal.

After several tense seconds, they heard the rattle of someone trying the door at the top of the staircase. Jones was glad that he had taken the precaution of locking both the top and bottom doors and turning off the lights. They had some extra seconds to prepare.

Automatic weapon fire told them when each of the doors to the stairs had been breached. Both detectives were veterans of previous gun battles, and waited with the nervous expectancy of knowing what was coming.

'No one else needs to be hurt!' a voice came from the stairway. 'Just turn over the Herbivore, his trollop, and their spawn to me for purification and everyone else can leave.'

'No can do, Ms. Sommerstone,' Wright said as he aimed he weapon toward the silhouette outlined in the light from the upper area of the stair. He hoped that his partner was doing the same. He had no hope that Janah would be willing to give herself up, but he felt honor-bound to give her the chance.

'Give yourself up and we'll get you the help you need,' he continued. 'Why destroy yourself and them?'

'Because they're evil!' Janah screamed. 'If they aren't destroyed, they'll continue to spread their poison just like their evil spawn is doing with that young girl right now!'

'You're the one who's full of poison, Janah!' Wright shouted back at her. 'I've known Herbie for more than ten years. I was at his wife's funeral after she had the stroke that killed her. No one could have faked the grief that he showed. Not being able to have children just added to the pain.'

'Lies!' Janah emptied the magazine of her gun, stepped back into the shadows, and placed a full one in its slot. 'I know that Cindy has had her hooks into him ever since middle school! She corrupted him, blinded him, took him away from me and had his child! She kept him from seeing any other girl! He would never have married anyone else!'

Stepping back out of the shadows, she began firing controlled shots in the direction she had heard the detective's voice. Jones, having stayed silent, aimed his service pistol at the woman's silhouette and squeezed off three shots.

As he heard her scream, Wright also fired off three quick shots in the direction of the stairs. There was a grunt of pain and the sound of something falling down the stairs. Both detectives waited and then saw Janah's shadowed form at the top of the stairs just before she disappeared. After a few moments to make sure that she was not in the house, or at least unable to present a danger, the two detectives cautiously mounted the stairs up to the ground level area.

The entire room had been riddled with bullets. On the floor behind the heavy overstuffed couch, they found Agent Polluck, unconscious and alive, but severely wounded. Nearer to the front door behind an upturned metal coffee table, they found the also badly wounded and unconscious Agent Seth.

As the detectives provided what emergency assistance they could, sirens and flashing lights could be heard and seen approaching the front yard. Placing his weapon back into its holster and holding his badge where it was obvious, Jones stepped outside onto the porch.

'Brookdale PD Detective Jones,' he identified himself. 'There are two severely wounded federal agents inside. The shooter is still at large, possibly wounded and definitely dangerous. My partner and four civilians are also inside. The civilians are downstairs in the panic room.'

One of the arriving deputies radioed for medical teams and additional personnel to begin a search of the area. Another deputy accompanied Jones back inside.

Wright had been able to stop the

bleeding of both agents, but they were still unconscious and exceedingly pale. Wright had also pulled the throw covers off of several chairs he had used as covers to keep the injured men warm.

'I think they have a chance of pulling through,' Wright opined guardedly, 'if we can prevent them from going into shock.'

'There were EMTs only five minutes behind us,' the deputy informed him. 'My partner has radioed for extra medical help. A full MD should arrive with them shortly.'

Jones went downstairs to turn on the lights and to give the password to Herbie and his group. At the bottom of the stairs and to one side, he found the weapon that Janah had used in her attack.

'No wonder her attack was so devastating!' he realized. 'She was a one-woman army!'

Jones pushed the intercom button and said, 'Lucy, I'm home!'

'What's happened, John?' Herbie's voice came from the speaker.

'The FBI agents are in a bad way,' Jones answered. 'George and I aren't injured and Janah has escaped for now. She may have been wounded. There's blood on the steps.'

There was a loud metallic click as the lock's bolt slid back and the door to the panic room opened.

'Things look pretty gruesome upstairs right now,' Jones told the group as they emerged. 'The weapon she used fell down the stairs after George and I opened fire at her silhouette. We heard her scream either in pain or in rage just before we saw her head back up the stairs.'

As they reached ground level, Wright greeted them with a grim expression on his face. 'The two deputies who reported finding the Escalade have been taken to the hospital with severe head wounds and badly bruised ribs. The tow truck should arrive soon to take her SUV to the yard for forensic evaluation.'

Polluck and Seth had been stabilized by the paramedics using IVs of electrolytes and other fluids to replace nutrients from the large loss of blood. As soon as the MD had declared them ready for transport, they were put onto gurneys and loaded into the ambulances to be taken to the hospital emergency room.

Because Johann and Jenny looked as if they were about to pass out, one of the medical technicians gave them a quick examination and declared that they were having a normal reaction to stress and seeing the two men so badly injured.

'From what they told me,' he said, 'they've been through more traumatic experiences in the last seventy-two hours than most people do in a lifetime. I'd recommend counseling. They're both strong personalities, and being able to talk about their feelings with one another should help them get through the major rough spots.'

'Thank you,' Cindy said. 'They've developed a strong rapport with one another over the last several days.'

'Having someone they've shared experiences and with who they can talk to can be a strong factor in recovery from a major trauma,' the technician agreed. 'Support from family members and adult friends is important, too.'

17

Janah was in extreme pain. The wounds in her left side and her right arm had finally stopped bleeding, but the pain had increased.

She couldn't understand why, when her mission was so righteous, that she kept failing.

After she had failed to eliminate Cindy and her family, the hated Herbivore had retracted his statement in *USA Today*, stating that he had made it under duress because of Cindy's kidnapping.

Now she had been wounded and had lost her weapon, all without accomplishing any part of her goal. Everyone kept telling her that what she *knew* had to be true was wrong, and that she was the one behaving in an irrational and evil manner.

The Junker she had taken from the rent-a-wreck lot had worked well enough to get her back to her time-share unit, where she had placed lots of tape and large pads on her wounds. That had absorbed the blood. The extra doses of pain relievers had done little, however; though she had finally fallen into a fitful sleep plagued with fever-induced night-mares of grinning devils' heads laughing at her and calling her demented, evil, and unworthy of her faith.

She awoke in a cold sweat and far from rested. 'Why am I being tormented this way?' she asked herself, but received no answer. 'I refuse to believe that I've gone crazy!'

After taking the full dosage of maximum-strength acetaminophen, she went to the bathroom to check and redress her wounds. The bullets appeared to have passed through the muscle tissues of her side and arm without causing serious arterial bleeding. She used an antibiotic antiseptic cream on the wounds, which showed no signs of infection, and placed sterile pads over them. Then she wrapped them in sterile gauze and adhesive tape to hold everything in place.

When she had finished, she went to the kitchen refrigerator and took out a bottle of drinking water and began to quench her thirst and cool her throat. She hoped that when she took her temperature later, she would have no more signs of fever.

Now, she told herself, *if I can just get some restful sleep!*

★ ★ ★

The replacements for Jeff Polluck and Jake Seth were due to arrive from the local FBI substation within hours.

'Now that we know that she has access to a place in Oak Leaf Acres,' Wright was suggesting, 'maybe we can wrap this case up before the new agents arrive. Johann, do you and Jenny think you could give us the approximate location if we got a map of the time-share resort?'

'I think we could put you close by,' Johann agreed after receiving a positive nod from Jenny. 'We walked along tree-lined paths to keep hidden, but we saw plenty of street signs. The gate was easy to see from where we were hidden.'

'The gate was controlled by a touch keypad,' Jenny told the detectives. 'We were able to squeeze through the bars, but an adult might be too big. Johann almost got stuck.'

'Did either of you notice a guard station?' Jones inquired. 'Any way of gaining entry without a pass code?'

'Not that I noticed.' Jenny frowned. 'Did you, Johann?'

Johann searched his memory for a moment. Then his eyes lit up. 'There was a phone box on the same pole as the keypad. It looked like a direct line to the visitors' center.'

'That could mean they have someone on duty to give guests of shareowners access to the grounds,' Herbie said. 'We may be able to convince someone to let us in.'

'You and Cindy,' Wright's stern voice reminded them, 'will take Jenny home to her frantically worried mother, and Johann needs to be away from potential violence. Department policy forbids us from knowingly placing civilians, especially minors, in jeopardy. The local sheriff's have agreed to escort you back to the Riverview city limits. There, uniforms

155

will continue to escort you to Jenny's home. We'll notify Ms. Norris that her daughter is safe and unharmed after they've shown us the place on the map where they were held and you're on your way. I mean it, Herbie! No heroics or delays. Go straight home. Do not pass go. Do not collect two hundred dollars.'

★ ★ ★

The two teenagers, exhausted by their adventures, had fallen asleep in the back seat of Herbie's car.

'It's good to see the kids finally relaxed,' Herbie commented, looking in the rearview mirror. 'I hope that Wright, Jones and company can capture Janah without further violence. She really needs counseling.'

'Do you think she'd ever be willing to let go of her fixations?' Cindy wondered. 'She's believed for most of her life that you and I were the reason for all of her losses and tragedies.'

'We can but hope and pray,' Herbie answered. 'She really needs to see her

156

choices. With everything that she's done, she'll probably never be released into normal society again. She's broken too many laws and endangered too many lives to be allowed her freedom.'

The Oak Leaf County sheriff's car turned off as a Riverview PD unit moved into position when they got to the city limits.

'So far,' Cindy commented as she viewed the exchange, 'everything seems to be going as planned.'

'I hope the same can be said about the time-share space.' Herbie's sad frown deepened.

The foursome was greeted by a relieved Mrs. McGruder and a nearly hysterical Mrs. Norris.

'You are *never* to leave this yard except to go to school, young lady,' Mrs. Norris said, reacting to the very frightening events of the last several hours. 'That horrible woman could have seriously harmed or even killed you! And you, young man, are not to come near my daughter!'

Before Jenny or anyone else could respond, Mrs. McGruder placed her hand lightly on Mrs. Norris's shoulder. 'Helen,' she said kindly but sternly, 'neither of these children nor their police guardians have done anything wrong. The children were less than two blocks away and the policewoman was only a hundred feet away from them. If you wish to place blame, place it on that sick woman where it belongs!'

Helen looked as if she was about to vent more angry words, and then she let out a deflating sigh. 'You're right, Rachel.' She looked at her daughter. 'I should be concentrating on having you back safely. This whole situation has had me in a state of panic.'

'That's only because you love me and care what happens to me, Mom.' Jenny placed her arms around her mother and gave her a hug. 'Some of the kids at school don't even have *one* parent who cares. I have you and Mrs. McGruder. And now I also have Mrs. Schmidt and Mr. Vore. I'm very fortunate.'

18

Detectives Wright and Jones followed the sheriff's detectives, giving them the lead because the time-share resort was a part of their jurisdiction.

'This matches the description of the place the kids said they were being held when they escaped,' Jones told the county detectives. 'State DMV records say that the clunker in the driveway is registered to a local rent-a-wreck company. The management is checking the yard and their recent rental records. They should be reporting back to us shortly.'

No movement had been detected inside the house and no lights could be seen from the street.

'Maybe she passed out from the pain of her wounds and the blood loss,' the older of the two sheriff detectives remarked. 'You say you believed she'd been shot?'

'The evidence was inconclusive,' Wright responded, 'but the probability was high.'

The lead detective's cell phone vibrated in his pocket. He answered and listened for a moment, then grunted a reply and disconnected.

'That was dispatch with word from the rent-a-wreck company,' he told them. 'They claim that the vehicle in question wasn't rented out recently and is missing from their lot. They're currently reporting it as stolen.'

'So now,' Wright proclaimed, 'we have probable cause to inspect the house?'

The sheriff's detective answered in the affirmative. 'But first, we check out the vehicle in the driveway for evidence that it's been part of a foul play scenario.'

The detectives cautiously approached the car. Using their high-intensity flash-lights, they were able to spot what appeared to be blood on the front seat and the driver's door handle.

'We have reason to believe there's a victim with serious wounds inside the house,' the lead detective said. 'Said victim could be in mortal danger from blood loss. We have a moral duty to enter the house and determine the situation.'

The detectives and the back-up deputies approached the house cautiously. The deputies circled around to watch the back of the house as the detectives knocked on the front door. After three tries, yet receiving no response, the lead sheriff's detective, whose name was Johnson, tried the door. It was unlocked, and opened readily.

'We do this by the numbers,' he said, drawing his gun. 'We still have no idea what we may find inside.'

With weapons at the ready, they entered the house, announcing themselves as they each checked a different area of the living room. After clearing the room, each detective checked a different room, continuing to call out that they were peace officers and inquiring if there was anyone in the house needing assistance.

Finally, Johnson called out from a back bedroom, 'In here! Call 911 for medical assistance! She's pale and her breathing is ragged and shallow, but she's still alive.'

The other officers were apprised of the situation and told to form a perimeter around the house as Detective Jones called the visitors' center to advise them that a medical response team was on its way and requested that the gate be opened. One of the deputies was assigned to meet them and to lead them to the injured person.

'She appears to be in a coma or severe shock,' Johnson told his partner, Sandy, as she talked to the 911 dispatcher. 'Because of the shock and pain, she may have accidentally OD'd on pain medication. She appears to have bandaged her wounds herself.'

Minutes later, the medical response team and their escort arrived, lights flashing and sirens screaming.

The med-techs quickly removed the wheeled stretcher from the back of the transport vehicle and were shown to the bedroom where Janah lay upon her bed.

The paramedics took Janah's vitals and reported to the doctors at the hospital. Following the doctors' instructions, they gave her IV insertions and placed an oxygen mask on her face. After a second check of Janah's vital signs indicated that she was stable, the med-techs placed her in the ambulance. As the ambulance was leaving, the forensic vehicles arrived.

'We need a quick check of the vehicle before it's towed to the impound yard,' Johnson instructed. 'Check the house for other signs of occupancy. Two minors may have been held in there before they managed to escape.'

'Our suspect has allegedly made other kidnapping attempts, causing severe bodily harm to local and federal officers,' Jones added.

★ ★ ★

The late-night television news broadcast gave a brief summary of the events of the day concerning the kidnapping of the two teenagers, the shoot-out at the safe house, and the finding of a wounded suspect at the time-share unit.

'Law enforcement personnel,' the newsperson summed up his report, 'have refused to reveal anything further, citing an on-going investigation.'

'At least that horrid and disturbed woman won't be stalking anyone for a long time,' Helen Norris commented as she turned off the television. 'Something must be terribly wrong with her mental and emotional wiring for her to have done all of the things you say she's done, Mr. Vore.'

Now that Helen had calmed down from her worries about her daughter, she showed a willingness to be forgiving and to try and understand the woman.

Herbie was glad Rachel had suggested they all should allow themselves time to process the last several days and work out their emotions.

'My late husband, Michael, was a psychologist,' she explained. 'He always believed that the best time to work out feelings was as soon as possible after a traumatic or painful experience.'

Rachel, Herbie, the Norrises, and the Schmidts had talked for hours after Rachel had made the suggestion. Since Herbie and Cindy knew the most about the past events leading up to the current events, they tended to field the most questions. The teens listened and offered their own stories and feelings. Helen was the most frightened and tended to have emotional outbursts. Rachel, having been married to a clinical psychologist for many years, was the calmest and least volatile of their little group.

Even so, the recent events had definitely taken their toll on her. She spoke in clipped sentences and seemed to take strength from the controlled environment. Noticing that several members showed signs of fatigue, she suggested that everyone go home and try to get some rest.

'We've all had a long, tiring and eventful day,' she told them, watching Johann and Jenny smothering yawns behind their hands. 'If anyone feels the need to talk more tomorrow, I know a couple of professionals willing to do emergency intervention.'

'Do you think you can drive all the way back to Brookdale?' Cindy inquired of Herbie.

'There's an inexpensive but clean and comfortable motel less than a mile from here,' he said. 'I'll get a room for the night. You have my cell number if you should need me.'

'Take care of yourself, my dear friend,' she said as she kissed his cheek.

19

At the hospital, Janah began to thrash and make incoherent noises. The nurse monitoring her room notified the attending physician and went into the room to check the life-sign recorders. When she arrived, Janah was attempting to remove her IV and monitoring attachments. She was still apparently unconscious but very agitated.

'No, you devils!' Janah finally yelled. 'I haven't completed my mission! You can't have me yet! I must remove the evil that is the Herbivore, Cindy and their illegitimate spawn!'

She sat up in bed, her eyes closed, and attempted to remove the covers. Still screaming, she clawed at the lines attached to her.

The doctor walked in as the nurse was attempting to calm Janah and get her to lie back down. The doctor immediately assessed the situation and prepared a sedative and injected the manic patient's IV bottle. Before the sedative took effect, Janah swung her arms, connecting to the doctor's jaw and knocking him back into the nurse. As they were untangling themselves and getting up from the floor, the officer on duty in the hall entered the room.

'Everything under control, Doc?' he inquired as he took in the scene.

'It is now,' the doctor reported, he and the nurse red-faced. 'The patient seems to have had a severe night terror. She's been sedated. I'm recommending restraints for the time being. If she has another episode, she may do harm to herself or others.'

★   ★   ★

Janah's mind knew that she had failed once again. She could not fathom how she could have been captured, restrained, and made so weak. She was doing righteous work. That was supposed to give her strength.

Subconsciously, she realized that she must have been near death when she had been hospitalized. She would rest and plan. Then she would escape and strike! She must allow herself to relax and heal as she put the visions from her night terror away in a small cell in her mind.

★ ★ ★

Detective Wright sat across from Herbie in the motel room. Herbie had contacted the detective early that morning, asking for anything new on Janah's condition.

'She apparently took an accidental overdose of pain medication while performing self-applied medical procedures on her bullet wounds. She also seems to have had a troubled night and needed to be restrained and sedated.'

Herbie shook his head as his friend reported the details of the night's events. 'The doctor and the nurse are okay?' he asked.

'The doctor's jaw is a nice shade of purple and the nurse was a little embarrassed when the hospital security guard came in as they were untangling themselves from the floor,' Wright said. 'Most of the injuries were to their dignities.'

Wright asked about Herbie's night.

'The six of us had an impromptu therapy session last night,' Herbie said after several moments of silence. 'We were still up when the news reported Janah's hospitalization.'

20

Janah's coma-induced dreams continued to plague her as the medications and restraints kept her body steady. Constant visions of her brother pleading with her to stop her useless vendetta reappeared. In her mind, he held out his arms and repeatedly shouted for an end to the blood-quest she was so determined to follow. As he stood there, a dead expression on his face, blood would appear to flow copiously from wounds all over his body, and then his arms and legs would fall away as if they had been chopped off. As they did, she could hear his voice shouting the words, 'No more! Not one drop more!'

The scene changed to grinning horned creatures with long shark's-tooth-shaped fangs that attempted to devour her. Extreme heat surrounded her so there was no escape. Then the dream would fade, only to repeat itself moments later.

The assault on Janah's mind was as devastating as it was unrelenting. As she felt herself weakening mentally and spiritually, a voice in the back of her mind said, 'Repent! So many people are telling you the same thing, proving the errors of your conceptions, saying that you have much to atone for in your recent actions. Repent and atone!'

'I've done nothing wrong!' her mind shouted back, banishing both the terrors she had been enduring and the gentle voice urging her to believe that which her whole body refuted violently.

With renewed commitment to her goal, she gradually gained the strength to banish her last doubts along with her coma. Her mind began to gain in strength, and her body gradually took on signs of increased healing and renewed health. Within the month, she was allowed to sit up in bed and be fed bland but solid food.

★   ★   ★

'The patient appears to be gaining strength as her wounds heal,' the doctor reported into his dictation recorder. 'However, she still thrashes violently at times as if she is fending off an attack of some kind. Her disturbed behavior previous to her being admitted makes me reluctant to allow her into the regular hospital population. Psychiatric evaluation of her current state of mind may prove valuable in her continued treatment.'

The doctor shut off his recorder and sat at his desk, his chin resting in his folded hands as he leaned forward thoughtfully, his elbows acting as support pins. Switching his Dictaphone back on, he continued, 'Patient exhibits almost no interest in her surroundings, but seems willing to be left in whatever position the nurses or orderlies leave her in. She appears to be the perfectly docile, nearly catatonic, subject. End current observations of patient Janah Sommerstone.'

The doctor sighed as he rubbed his recently healed jaw. Then he went to place the Dictaphone on his secretary's desk to be transcribed.

★ ★ ★

Cindy was visiting with Helen and Rachel, sharing the neighborhood gossip and enjoying getting to know her close neighbors.

'Jenny is excited about entering high school when the new school year begins,' Helen was telling them. 'The new curriculum and new students from the other middle schools is just about all she can talk about, except for your Johann, Cindy. Either she sees him as an older brother, or she's having her first crush. I don't know which makes me more uncomfortable. She seems to be growing up so fast!'

'Isn't Jenny's birthday next week, Helen?' Rachel inquired, changing the subject. 'After the last few weeks, perhaps a 'grown-up' party with music, punch, dancing, and adult hosts and hostesses catering the food and cake might help relieve some of the stress.'

'That sounds wonderful,' gushed Helen. 'And didn't you tell me that Johann recently turned sixteen? Why not have a double party? Sixteen's a special birthday.'

'Let's check with the kids and get their input,' Cindy responded. 'They may have their own ideas as to guest invites and activities. They may even have a special place where they'd like to have their party.'

'Okay,' Rachel said, 'I'll sound the kids out on the subject and we can go from there.'

Rachel found Jenny and Johann in front of his house, looking as though the world had stopped spinning, and feeling let down now that the excitement seemed to be over.

'Why so glum, chums?' Rachel asked as she approached them. 'You've both helped to capture a dangerous person, survived being kidnapped, and have each found a special friend. I'd say that a lot for two young people.'

'I guess all of those detective novels don't talk about one feeling — like everything's stopped after the case is solved,' Jenny sighed. 'Mrs. McGruder, how do we get back to being normal after all we've been through and experienced?'

'Yeah,' Johann agreed. 'It's like we're not the same people anymore.'

'Maybe getting back into feeling normal,' Rachel began, 'is just doing normal things again. Like shopping for back-to-school things, birthday parties, going for walks, watching TV, sharing ideas and dreams with best friends, doing the things that feel important and real. Going out and making memories.'

Rachel looked at the two young people as if she had just had an idea. 'I know! Why not have a victory celebration?' she suggested. 'Or even just an old-fashioned double birthday party? I hear that Johann had his sixteenth birthday not long ago. And Jenny, isn't your fourteenth birthday coming up soon?'

Both young people looked at each other, then at Rachel. A look of understanding passed between them as Johann spoke. 'Why not have a heroes' party at the children's wing at the hospital for all of the seriously ill kids? Wouldn't those kids enjoy being recognized as the heroes they truly are?'

'We could invite their parents and the hospital support staff,' Jenny said, enthused. 'Their support should be rewarded, too.'

'I think that's a wonderful idea,' Rachel agreed as she quickly thought about who she would have to talk to in order to set everything up. 'I have some friends at the hospital I'll need to talk to, but I'm sure we can get them to agree.'

Rachel, Johann, Jenny went over suggestions for setting up the entertainment and decorations. Later, as Rachel told Cindy and Helen of the suggestion that Johann and Jenny had made, she remarked, 'Those two are among the most giving and unselfish young people I've ever met. They'll leave their mark on this world that will be for the better.'

'May others follow in their footsteps,' Cindy and Helen agreed.

★ ★ ★

Word of the impending Celebration of Courage for the seriously and terminally ill children in the pediatric ward reached Janah through the hospital's gossip grapevine. Janah also learned that the anonymous sponsors were the very people she had reviled and hated for all of her adult life. The words 'Repent' and 'Atone' grew louder and louder in her mind.

'They are the ones who need to repent and atone!' she shouted loud enough that a muscular and concerned-faced orderly rushed into the room, the security guard with him, to check on her.

'Calm down, Ms. Sommerstone,' he said soothingly. 'You don't want to return to the restraints, do you? Just relax and tell me what's upsetting you.'

Janah appeared to relax, but refused to speak with the orderly.

Shrugging his shoulders, the he turned to leave, stopped and said, 'If you change your mind, press your call button. Someone will arrive quickly and you can tell them whatever you need.'

21

In his fictional story about the real-life mystery he had lived through, Herbie related how the upcoming Celebration of Courage had come about.

'In spite of all the hatred and evil that had been directed at them,' he wrote, 'Yancy and Nancy still sought to bring joy into the lives of others. The Serious and Terminally Ill Children's Ward buzzed with expectation and even, in many cases, renewed hope for the future. Smiles were on the faces of the young patients as the doctors and nurses reminded them that their courage in the face of all of their pain truly made them superheroes.'

What will Happen to Cindy? had now grown to fill at least two thirds of the blank lined pages that had been bound in the package he had received seemingly a lifetime ago. The FBI agents who had come to take the places of the wounded Polluck and Seth had taken statements from the Brookdale and Riverview Police Departments and the Oak Leaf County Sheriff's Department. They had also interviewed the various persons and agencies involved in solving the kidnappings.

All of the injured law enforcement officers were expected to make full physical recoveries. Janah's physical recovery was also advancing as expected. She still had numerous outbursts that seemed to have nothing to do with anything else. The doctors told the FBI that she probably would never recover enough of her mental abilities to the point where she could stand trial.

The agents reported to their superiors and requested periodic updates on her condition and fitness for prosecution.

'I've never personally come across a case like this one.' The lead agent shook her head. 'At least three different kidnapping attempts, a murder, at least half a dozen law enforcement officers from four different agencies injured, most of them seriously, and several attempted murders. This is person is vicious and very disturbed. I hope we've seen the end of her rampage.'

The hospital's resident psychologist agreed. 'Even if she's pronounced cured, conviction of any of the crimes attributed to her would most likely keep her away from society for most of the rest her natural life.'

With that, the agents went to check on their colleagues.

The next day, at noon, was the Celebration of Courage event. Besides the current patients, several former patients were invited. Food and drink were served, stories of the physical therapies and innovative treatments many of the former patients had undergone were told.

'Many of the treatments used today were once last-ditch efforts or brand new and still experimental,' one doctor told the audience, 'but their successes gave us hope, and the results are here with us today. Thanks to them, we have given, and will continue to give, the hope of a healthier future to our youngest patients.'

Herbie stood beside Johann, Jenny, their mothers, and Rachel McGruder as the speeches continued.

'These kids and their parents are the

real-life superheroes,' Helen Norris remarked. 'They may never wish to see a doctor again, but they'll appreciate what they can sometimes accomplish. They make me ashamed of some of the ways in which I behaved recently.'

'Your behavior was understandable, Helen,' Mrs. McGruder told her. 'Any truly concerned parent would have been in a state of panic during what you and Cindy endured.'

The party ended on a high note a short time later when the hospital caterers brought out the refreshments and the attendees had a chance to get acquainted.

*   *   *

Janah's guard sat in a chair outside her door in the hallway reviewing the notes from the previous shifts. Her outbursts of the night before had been duly logged, and the orderly's report to the person on guard duty was placed in an incident report.

'Basically a quiet night,' he said to himself.

The day nurse said hello to him as she

went into Janah's room to give medicines and to chart Janah's progress. The room was quite at first, and then there was a loud crash. The guard pushed his alarm and rushed into the room. He found the day nurse getting up from a debris-filled floor.

'Where is she?' the guard questioned as he looked around for any place a person could hide. There were no visible hiding places, nor was there another exit to be seen. 'Did you see where she went?'

A whimper from the corner of the room behind the door caught the guard's attention. The whimper changed to a growl as an overturned cabinet was shoved away. Behind the cabinet as it was rolled over, Janah writhed on the floor and foamed at the mouth.

The nurse went to the emergency call button and told the floor nurses what had happened and in which room help was needed.

*   *   *

As the medical care workers and the parents at the Celebration of Courage were sharing stories with one another after the critically ill children were returned to their rooms, a worried-looking male nurse approached Herbie and a lab-coated man.

'Do either of you know where the attending physician for the patient in Room 407 of the dangerously disturbed wing is?' he asked. 'We've had an incident and need him, stat.'

The lab-coated man said, 'I'm the resident psychologist in that ward. Doctor Smith is the attending physician. If he's not handling an emergency, you should be able to reach him on his pager.'

'We've been trying to reach him, but he hasn't responded yet,' the nurse reported. 'However, you're needed also. The patient apparently has had some sort of physical breakdown and a psychotic episode.'

The doctor followed the nurse as Herbie went to find Cindy.

'Something has happened to Janah,' he told Cindy after finding her talking with several doctors about her own experience with a debilitating injury.

Cindy excused herself from her conversation and followed Herbie. As they walked to room 407, Herbie related the message that the nurse had given him and the psychologist.

'He said nothing about what happened?' Cindy inquired.

'Nothing more than the fact that Doctors Smith and Stafford were need in Janah's room.'

When they reached it, there were two guards, one on either side of the door. The day guard recognized them and held out his hand.

'I'm sorry, Mr. Vore, Ms. Schmidt, he told them, 'but both of the doctors have ordered that no one be allowed in.'

'Are they still inside with her?' Cindy nodded toward the locked door. 'If so, we'll wait out here for a while.'

The guard answered Cindy's question thoughtfully. 'Two agents and two detectives are on their way. I suppose it'll be all right for you to stay in the waiting area until then if the doctors haven't finished by that time.'

★   ★   ★

While they waited, Herbie said to himself, 'I'd still like to know how those notes and cards got delivered with no one noticing.'

'What did you say?' Cindy asked.

'Just thinking out loud. Did Janah have another accomplice other than John? How did all of those messages get by our neighbors, often in broad daylight? Whoever delivered them was like a wraith. When the envelope with those pictures was put through my mail slot, I was home, and I got to the window fairly quickly. The person had already vanished from sight, and had left no trace.'

'Until we know who and how, this won't be over, will it, Herbie?' Cindy responded.

'No, I don't think it will be. If someone's been aiding Janah and her brother, I think their agenda is still in operation. And we have no idea what that may be.'

Dr. Stafford walked into the waiting area as Cindy and Herbie had fallen into a thoughtful silence.

'Janah's apparently had a seizure of some type while having a psychotic episode,' he told them without preamble. 'Dr. Smith has given her a general anti-seizure medicine and a shot to calm down her mental stimuli.'

'Any indication as to what happened to bring on the symptoms?' Cindy wanted to know.

'We don't know for sure what brought on the seizure,' Dr. Stafford replied, 'but we do know that she was having troubling dreams quite often. Perhaps one of those triggered the seizure. Between it and the night terrors, she became violent and incoherent until she collapsed. The guard told us he found her, the nurse, and the room in an extremely disheveled state.'

Since no one but the medical and mental care personnel would be allowed into Janah's room until further notice, Herbie and Cindy decided to return to the area of the party. Finding that nearly everyone had left, they checked the floor's cafeteria for their friends. Seeing them at a corner table, they brought them up to date on the recent events and Herbie's theory of third-party involvement.

'Sounds like Ms. Sommerstone has a

ton of problems,' Jenny commented. 'Someone really failed to help her when she needed it.'

'And someone else may have used her pain and confusion to their own ends,' Johann added. 'I can't say that her behavior of late has endeared me to her, but I can't help pitying her.'

'Can either of you think of someone who might have had reason to wish ill of either of the two of you,' Rachel asked, 'or to the Sommerstones?'

'Outside of their church associates,' Herbie answered, 'I don't remember the Sommerstones socializing with anyone. They did have a reputation for being strict, but honest and fair, in their everyday affairs. The main thing I heard as a complaint against them was that they were hard people to cheat, but if someone succeeded, they never forgot, nor forgave. And they never dealt with that individual again.'

'I also heard that if there was a legal and non-violent way of paying such an offender back,' Cindy added, 'they'd find it and use it.'

'So,' Rachel summed up, 'we're looking at a family that was unsociable, fair, honest, unforgiving of wrongs done to them, and vindictive if it could be done legally and non-violently. Something and/or someone caused Janah to take those mores and warp them.'

'An evil person indeed,' agreed Helen.

22

The following weekend was the one of the last before school started, so Herbie had invited his friends, old and new, over for an end-of-summer picnic and barbeque at his home.

'I haven't done any real entertaining since Julie passed away,' he told everyone. 'Perhaps it's time I did more socializing.'

The big day arrived with pleasant temperatures and clear skies. Herbie's grill was ready to cook when his quests pulled up in front of his house.

'Perfect timing,' he told them. 'The grill's ready for the meat. Make yourselves comfortable out back on the patio.'

While Herbie took the hamburger patties, wieners, and other items to be cooked from the refrigerator, everyone found a place around the picnic table or on the lounges on the patio. The pleasant odors of grilling meat soon filled the air.

'I remember a few summer picnics in

the park where you grilled a lot of food for our friends from school. It was always cooked to perfection and everyone had fun playing softball and volleyball afterwards,' Cindy remarked as they ate. 'There was one guy, though, who was kinda shy.'

'Short and a bit nerdy?' Herbie asked.

'Yeah,' Cindy answered. 'A likeable nerd, though, and always willing to help you understand what the teacher had to say in class, or to help you with your homework. He was better than most of the teachers at explanations.'

'Wasn't his nickname Nerdy Jameson?' Herbie remarked, remembering the young man. 'He didn't like that name any more than I did mine. I think that you and I were two of the few people who always called him by his proper name.'

'You and Sam did have that in common, Herbie,' Cindy agreed with him.

As everyone enjoyed their meals, Herbie thought back to his high school days and his recollections of Sam Jameson. He was an intelligent young man with sandy hair and blue eyes; an unusual but pleasing combination with his light coffee-colored skin. Short and non-athletic, but not a physical weakling, Sam was uneasy in a crowd, but likeable and gregarious in small groups.

I haven't thought about him in ages, Herbie reflected. *He always seemed so meek. I wonder what he's been doing since high school.*

Herbie went to his bookshelves after everyone had gone home and pulled his senior yearbook from the section of memorabilia. He found the picture of Sam and the short biographical statement that was inside.

'Sam is a four-year member of the State's Scholarship Federation with a lifetime grade point average of 3.8,' he read. 'Sam has interests in botany, holistic medicine, and the body's reactions to its environment.'

Herbie opened his laptop and typed in Sam's full name, 'botany,' 'holistic medicine,' and 'physical reactions to the environment' into his search engine. Next, he worked on narrowing the number of hits by adding the words 'recent reports and studies of.' By continually refining his search, he finally was able to narrow the number of hits to a manageable number.

I'm sure that Johann could have done this quicker, he told himself, *but he doesn't have the feel for Sam's personality that Cindy and I have.* Sam enjoyed private research and experimentation.

Herbie chose the articles that sounded as if they would have attracted Sam's attention or that had his name listed as the author or co-author. On the most recent article, Herbie clicked on Sam's name to see what biographical information was available. Herbie was surprised to learn that Sam had disappeared after leaving an out-of-state convention nearly a year before.

'I've lost touch with a lot of people since I graduated high school,' he said aloud. 'I'm glad the reunion's coming up soon.'

Deciding that he had a resource that he wasn't utilizing, he drove to Cindy's and Johann's the next day.

'You sounded so mysterious on the phone this morning,' Cindy said when she answered Herbie's knock. 'Johann's got his laptop set up in the utility room.'

'I found some interesting things about Sam Jameson on the internet last night,' he explained. Then he told her about his searches of his old yearbook and of the internet. 'The author's bio claimed that he's been missing for about a year.'

Cindy led Herbie to the back area of the house where Johann was waiting.

'Hey, Yancy,' Herbie greeted him. 'You ready to 'gofer' an info run for me?'

'My 'puter's ready to go, Mack,' Johann replied.

Herbie gave Johann the printouts he had made from his research, and Johann typed in the addresses individually from the sheets of paper and carefully studied each page. He sighed, stretched, and then with several keystrokes found a long biography on one of the encyclopedia websites for the correct Samuel Johnson, PhD in botany, biology, and biochemistry.

'It says here — ' Johann pointed to lines of print as he spoke. ' — that he believed the human body could be made to react with the chemical properties of its environment in such a way that it'd behave like a chameleon. That would've been useful in warfare and espionage, except for the extremely adverse reactions of the subject's life-sustaining systems and mental stability.'

'Does the article give details of the symptoms?' Herbie inquired. 'Could Janah's behavior and her actions at the hospital have been from her experimenting with Sam's theories?'

A few more keystrokes, and Johann shook his head. 'Everything I'm finding out is either protected at the highest levels, or is inconclusive. I'm shutting down before someone from the Secret Service or Homeland Security notices my searches.'

'I don't think that'll help, Johann,' Herbie told him. 'These new FBI agents have been too interested in Janah's symptomatic behavior. They've been talking a lot to other alphabet departments in D. C. I'm sure our government were the people who helped Sam disappear.'

'Shades of the conspiracy novelists!' Johann exclaimed. 'That's just a little too weird for me.'

Cindy entered the room, a frown of disbelief and a look of shock on her face.

194

'The hospital just called,' she told them. 'Janah just passed away.'

'After her last episode.' Herbie let out a sigh. 'We were expecting that.'

'That's not all,' Cindy continued. 'They want to talk to us. An elder from her church, the FBI, and several people from a bunch of government agencies are all arguing about custody of the body.'

'Secret Service and HSD?' Johann asked. 'Are they among them?'

'I don't know, son,' Cindy replied. 'Why would they be involved?'

'Because of what Sam was working on when he disappeared,' Herbie answered. He gathered up his papers and gestured for Johann to give his laptop to him. 'It's better that they don't know that the computer belongs to you,' he said. 'Is there anything you need from the hard drive?'

'The programs I use and my school-work are automatically placed on my external hard drive, as well as my e-mail,' Johann answered, knowing what Herbie was implying. 'I don't belong to anything like Facebook or Twitter or to any of the online chat sites. TMI is more trouble than it worth.'

'Okay,' Herbie acknowledged, 'then perhaps they'll believe this is mine. If it's confiscated, I'll replace it.'

Herbie placed the laptop and his printouts in his car and took them to the hospital, thinking, *If I had had any idea what kind of trouble I was getting myself, Cindy and Johann into, I would've insisted that we use my computer.*

When Herbie arrived at the hospital, he went up to Janah's room, where he convinced the government people to speak with him privately.

'I think I've found information that will interest you,' he began, 'in relation to Janah Sommerstone and a missing scientist named Samuel Jameson.'

'And why do you think they're related, Mr. Vore?' Agent Shirley Quinn, the current lead for the FBI, asked with a hard tone in her voice. 'I don't see how the cases are connected.'

'Dr. Jameson was working on sensitive theories at the time he disappeared, Agent Quinn,' Agent Seymore from the Secret

Service informed her. 'He hadn't finished his experiments before he went missing. They proved to be extremely dangerous to the volunteer subjects. When he vanished about a year ago, the scientific and intelligence communities, in the vernacular of the last third of the twentieth century, 'had a cow'.'

'HSD has been very active in attempting to find him and his lab notes,' a man with coppery skin, high cheekbones, and thick black hair named Walker Simpson spoke up. 'What he was working on could make 9/11 look like child's play if discovered by a hostile foreign power.'

'Having spies, soldiers, and saboteurs with the abilities of the chameleon would be extremely detrimental to the nation at war without those abilities against one that did,' Herbie interjected. 'What kind of defense could be mounted against such a bio-weapon?'

'Where did you get your information?' Walker gave him a stony look. 'That's supposed to be highly classified.'

'We went to high school and community college together.' Herbie grinned at the Homeland Security agent. 'I knew his interests better than any of our classmates. I used notes from our senior yearbook to set up special search parameters and then used my knowledge about him to see what he'd been doing since that time. ''If you know what you're looking for and how to phase your search question, you can find out almost anything on the internet.'' Herbie smiled to himself as he quoted Johann from their first meeting.

Shirley looked at him with renewed respect as she asked, 'What have you found out that the government doesn't know?'

'Almost everything that doesn't have a government lock-out,' Herbie answered. 'My computer skills are good, but not so good that I can hack into government secrets.'

'Show us your notes and tell us your theories and reasons for your interests,' Seymore ordered. 'Leave nothing out!'

Herbie related all of the things that had happened over the summer: how written communications had arrived at his and Cindy's mail slots without a postmark or a return address, leaving no evidence of how they had been delivered and no one spotting the person or persons making the deliveries.

'Brookdale and Riverview detectives could find no forensic evidence on any of the materials delivered. Not even on the book of blank lined pages from FedEx Kinko's,' he finished, and set the print-outs and the book on the table in front of him. 'As a writer, I decided to record all of the events as a fictional mystery thriller on the blank pages of the book I was sent. Observations, questions, etcetera of the major participants have all been recorded. I've made guesses about some of the conversations and motivations of which I have no specific knowledge. They were what I believed to be plausible, from what the later events revealed.'

'And what about your findings of Dr. Jameson's research?' HSD agent Simpson asked.

'All on the history of this laptop.'

'We also need to talk with Ms. Schmidt and her son,' Agent Sayles, the other FBI agent, stated. 'They may know more than they realize.'

* * *

Herbie was told that Johann's laptop and his laptop would eventually be returned. It would take at least six weeks before the computer forensics team gleaned everything they could from the two computers.

'Don't expect all of your files to still be there when they're returned to you,' he was told. 'Anything pertaining to Dr. Jameson or his work will be permanently deleted and unrecoverable once we've recorded all of the information we want.'

Herbie gave a mental shrug and gave the federal agents the scowl that they expected from a citizen whose property was being confiscated. He did not intend to use his computer again, nor did he want Johann to use his. There was too much chance of a tracking program having been secretly installed. The rights of the private citizen were supposed to be inviolate, but as the saying went, 'national security trumps all.'

Having told Detectives Wright and Jones of his findings on the internet and of his suspicions in relation to much of

Janah's latest behaviors, he gave them the parameters he believed would be helpful to the toxicology tests.

'If I'm correct, it may explain some of the early planting of the notes without any evidence being left behind,' he told them. 'Sam was a brilliant theorist and was willing to take excessive risks to prove a point true or false. From what I heard them arguing back and forth about, the feds don't think his disappearance was voluntary. Or if it was, then they believe that he must have defected.'

'And maybe he was kidnapped and when they either got what they wanted, or when he refused to divulge his secrets, they killed him,' Detective Wright hypothesized. 'Or they eliminated him after his defection had given them all that they wanted.'

23

Herbie replaced Johann's laptop just before the start of the new school year.

'The first thing I want you to do,' Herbie told Johann, 'is to make sure all of the hard drives belonging to you or your mother are as secure and defensible from cyber-attacks as you can make them. Next, I'd like you to check all of my backups before they're reinstalled, and then place those same safeguards on my computer and my new external hard drive. I don't want anyone, and I do mean *anyone*, invading my privacy. And I want you and Cindy to be protected to the best of our abilities. The ability of anyone, especially the government, to find out the most intimate details of my life, or those of people I care about, really scares me at times.'

'Jenny's mom just gave her a laptop of her own for her birthday,' Johann stated. 'I was going to set it up later. I'll tell her and Mrs. Norris that as long as I'm upgrading the security on my computer, I could do the same for them.'

'If Mrs. McGruder has a computer,' Herbie said thoughtfully, 'offer to upgrade hers too.'

The next weekend, Herbie received a note printed in childish block letters through his mail slot. This time there was no envelope and the note was unsigned.

'It's not over until it's over!' the note said.

Herbie rushed outside immediately. The late afternoon sun was situated behind his house, with the shadows providing sharp contrasts between light and dark. Looking up and down the street, he noticed that several leaves on the hedge at his property line were bending in the opposite direction of the wind.

Stop, Sam!' he shouted. 'If that's you, please stop and talk to me.'

'What happened to Janah,' a voice out of the air sobbed, 'wasn't my fault! She found out about my experiments and stole several doses of the serum made from my original, unperfected, formula. I tried to warn her of the dangerous side effects, but she laughed and used it anyway. She said she'd make you and Cindy pay for your crimes and then punish everyone from our old school. She claimed that what happened during prom night in that old horror film was nothing compared to the devastation she'd wreak upon her brother's class reunion.'

'What happened when she used the serum?' Herbie inquired of the sobbing, disembodied voice. 'She never seemed to blend in with her surroundings as you appear to be doing.'

'It wore off in a few hours,' the voice said. 'Even when she tried it a week and then a month later, the result was the same. The major change was the increased viciousness in her personality. She began to rant insanely about revenge, and how Cindy had stolen you away from her. I faked my disappearance and worked on my formula in secret. I thought I'd perfected it, so I used it on myself. Too late, I found out that this time the effect appeared irreversible. I almost went mad trying to find a way. I knew that I had to warn you about Janah. I learned that Cindy and her son had moved back into the area. I heard Janah's obscene and threatening phone calls while standing close enough to touch her at the phone booth. The only way I could warn either of you was to set up the notes and cards in such a way as to make you take her seriously.'

'So,' Herbie mused, 'you were the one who delivered all of the missives?'

'No, she delivered the photographs and sent the book of blank pages,' he commented. 'She used the old formula right before she approached your house and slipped the envelope through your mail slot.'

'Have you been able to notice any other effects from the serum made with the new formula?' Herbie inquired.

'I used it over six months ago, and I haven't returned to normal. Janah became obsessed with revenge, while I've become obsessed with being normal again. During the last two months, I've gotten physically weaker and very weary. I theorize that the constant changes are taking an immense toll on my physical reserves.'

'And the notes and other things you've

handled,' Herbie said, perplexed, 'how is it that they're visible and readable?'

'Unless I'm in constant contact with something, it remains normal. As to why something I'm holding or wearing takes on the properties of a chameleon, I have no answer. The only theory I have is that somehow the changes in my body chemistry are only able to affect anything I come into physical contact with for as long as I'm touching it.'

Sam entered into a convulsive sounding fit of coughing.

'The coughs are getting worse,' he continued. 'I've destroyed all of my notes and theories and left a confession in a locked box in my room at the laboratory where I was teaching and working at the time that I disappeared. I used an old storage closet there to hide my papers after Janah had stolen most of the original solution I made. I didn't want her to know I was working on an improved formula. Nor did I wish for her to know that, when we were in high school, I had a crush on her. The person she became after the lynching of her folks changed those feelings to ones of pity. I went to the city college like you, and then transferred to one of the state universities. I returned to do grad work and to teach biochemistry at the local campus. She was doing work of her own there and staying with her brother. She learned of my work, used a sample, and then stole the rest. After Cindy and her son moved to Riverview, she became obsessed with destroying the two of you. What has happened since then, you know.

The sound of the debilitating cough once again rang through the empty air. This time, there was a slight flicker that momentarily revealed the form of a man.

'I don't think I have much time left,' Sam remarked as he fought to control the coughs. 'Please, destroy any notes and remnants of the formula I may have over-looked. Then give my confession to the proper authorities. My work is too danger-ous to allow it to be used. Promise me you'll do as I ask!'

As Sam went into another round of spasmodic coughing, Herbie promised. He truly believed he was making a promise to a dying man. 'On which campus and in which laboratory is your room?' he asked.

'The main campus of Riverview in Chemlab #3. My room was the third door on the left. The storage closet is hidden behind a mirrored wall in back. The top right corner has a release catch. Press hard and it'll open.'

With a last choking cough, Sam visibly spewed blood on the ground and slowly became visible as he died.

Herbie pulled Sam's body under the hedge. He knew that to keep his promise to destroy any experimentation notes and solutions, notification of Sam's death and resting place would have to wait for an hour.

The room and storage closet had been easy to locate. Herbie took everything that he found, bundled it up, and took it home. There he used his paper shredder and burned everything in his incinerator to complete the destruction of all that he had found except the folder labeled 'Confession of Samuel Jameson.'

After he stirred the ashes to make sure

that it had all been consumed, he called Detective Wright, told him most of the story, and asked that a morgue vehicle be sent to his house.

'I don't want any trouble,' Herbie finally said, 'but I made Sam certain promises before he died. I intend to keep them.'

The agents from the FBI, Secret Service, and HSD were not happy with Herbie, but since Sam had declared that the notes and formula had been destroyed in his written confession, they knew that they would have to be satisfied.

An official autopsy was made as an inquiry into the cause of death with the hope that chemical residues might reveal insights into Sam's formula. None were found.

We do hope that you have enjoyed reading this large print book.

Did you know that all of our titles are available for purchase?

We publish a wide range of high quality large print books including:
Romances, Mysteries, Classics
General Fiction
Non Fiction and Westerns

Special interest titles available in large print are:
The Little Oxford Dictionary
Music Book, Song Book
Hymn Book, Service Book

Also available from us courtesy of Oxford University Press:
Young Readers' Dictionary
(large print edition)
Young Readers' Thesaurus
(large print edition)

For further information or a free brochure, please contact us at:
Ulverscroft Large Print Books Ltd.,
The Green, Bradgate Road, Anstey,
Leicester, LE7 7FU, England.
Tel: (00 44) **0116 236 4325**
Fax: (00 44) **0116 234 0205**